REVENGE INCORPORATED

With the accidental death of her doctor husband, twenty-five year-old Laura Kilburn's world collapsed. Then the anonymous letter came, offering information about the accident. A train ticket was enclosed. Intrigued, Laura soon found herself involved with a secret international organisation of wealthy and powerful men, dedicated to the righting of wrong. This is the story of Laura's exciting apprenticeship in the bizarre organisation known as Revenge Incorporated.

Warwickshire County Council

WOL 7.10	Willott Ho		
27. 08. 10	AVON		
Buck			
28. SEP 10.		2. JAN 2013	
08. JAN 11.	19-2-13.		
02. MAR 11			
04 JUL 11			
31. AUG 11	17 DEC 2018		
BHT			
10/11			

This item is to be returned or renewed before the latest date above. It may be borrowed for a further period if not in demand. **To renew your books:**

- **Phone the 24/7 Renewal Line 01926 499273 or**
- **Visit www.warwickshire.gov.uk/libraries**

Discover • Imagine • Learn • *with libraries*

 **Warwickshire** County Council

Working for Warwickshire

0132081182

DENNIS PHILLIPS

———————◆———————

REVENGE
INCORPORATED

Complete and Unabridged

LINFORD
Leicester

First published in Great Britain

First Linford Edition
published 1998

British Library CIP Data

Phillips, Dennis
    Revenge Incorporated.—Large print ed.—
Linford mystery library
1. Detective and mystery stories
2. Large type books
I. Title
823.9'14 [F]

ISBN 0–7089–5225–9

Published by
F. A. Thorpe (Publishing) Ltd.
Anstey, Leicestershire
Set by Words & Graphics Ltd.
Anstey, Leicestershire
Printed and bound in Great Britain by
T. J. International Ltd., Padstow, Cornwall

This book is printed on acid-free paper

1

Rain spattered suddenly against the train window, and the girl in the corner seat stared out into the anonymous night. On her lap a book lay open, but she hadn't turned a page in twenty miles. In the glass she could see the reflection of a man on the other side of the compartment. He too had a book, held up close to his face, but behind it he was taking more than a passing interest in her legs. She turned her head towards him and inspected him coolly and deliberately. At once his eyes swivelled back to the printed page.

Not that she was afraid of the man. If he made any movement which did not meet with her full approval, she might well break his arm, or worse. It would depend on what he did. The man did not know what was going through her mind, or he would have given his full attention to what he was reading. All he could see was a girl, beautiful rather than merely pretty. She had short copper-gold hair which gleamed under the dim lights, a strong face with high cheekbones as though there might be some Red Indian lurking in her bloodstream. She wore a green leather coat over a black dress which rode well up over her knees, revealing slim and well-shaped legs disappearing into fur boots. She appeared to be about twenty-five years old, and there was something in the face, something which was not quite bitterness, yet harsher than sadness. She was a woman a man would look at, any man. It would be expecting too much to ask a man on a late train not to sneak an occasional glance. A man would wonder too, why she should be alone. Certainly it was from her own choice. A woman like that need never be alone if she wished it otherwise. Ah, there was the letter again. She must have read it four times already, at least.

She unfolded the single sheet and stared at it. Although she knew the contents by heart she felt a compulsion to read the typed words again. It was a short letter

'Dear Mrs. Kilburn,
    If you would like to know more about your late husband's unfortunate death, and are interested in employment more suited to your temperament, use the enclosed ticket on the 11.47 train from Paddington tonight.'

It was unsigned. When the square anonymous envelope had arrived at the flat that morning, she had at first dismissed it as some kind of cruel practical joke. When John had died there had been a minor flood of letters of condolence and sympathy from friends and strangers alike. But even then, at the time of her ultimate misery, there had been one or two of a different kind. Unspeakable, diseased messages that had shaken her to the very depths. As the day wore on, she had found herself staring repeatedly at the white envelope on the hall table. She had read it again, and then again, dismissing it each time with reduced assurance. On impulse she telephoned Paddington and learned there was indeed an 11.47 p.m. train to Pumpleigh. She thought about going to the police, but decided against it. And now the punched ticket rested in her pocket. In another few minutes she would reach her destination. As to what would happen when she arrived, she hadn't the remotest idea. The whole thing was probably some kind of pointless hoax.

"Will you have a cigarette?"

She looked up quickly at the face behind the outstretched silver case. Well, he was harmless enough. It had taken him over an hour to think up that brilliant stratagem. Shaking her head, she said:

"Thank you, no. I don't smoke."

It was a lie. She did smoke sometimes. But if she accepted she would automatically accept his conversation, and that she did not want. Coupled with the chatter would be his clumsy attempts to pick her up, and she did not want that either. The man took his rebuff with a smile.

"Do you mind if I do?"

"I'm reading," she said acidly.

It was almost true. Once again the book was tilted towards her face, and once again she read the line at the top of page two. She had read that line almost as many times as she had the letter. But it served its purpose. The man retired behind his double screen of book and cigarette, muttering some embarrassed apology.

Minutes later the train began to lose speed. Laura Kilburn closed her book thankfully and peered out of the window. In the distance a tiny cluster of lights loomed out of the darkness and rushed towards the oncoming train. There was a hiss of brakes, and sudden voices in the corridor outside. She stood up as the train slowed to a halt. The man peered over his book almost shyly.

"Goodnight."

She took no notice, slid back the door and stepped out into the corridor. The rain was not heavy. There were a few people getting off the train, one or two boarding. It was one of those microcosms of life inseparable from a railway journey. At the moment of arrival, the platform suddenly busy with people. Getting off, getting on, welcoming the incoming, waving away the outgoing. The whole thing would last a few minutes. Then, quite suddenly, they would all have gone, the train swallowed up by the night, and people left behind scuttling in all directions as though to avoid any contact with other humans. All, that is, except the ticket-collector. He would be there, planted firmly beside his little gate, peering intently at the small tickets, beneath some inadequate lamp.

Laura looked hopefully at the few people on the platform, standing in the light so she would not be missed. Nor was she, not by any of the men on that damp station. But none of them approached her. Doors began to slam, there was a shout from the end of the platform, and a lamp swung to and fro. The train took its first tentative lurch forward, then gathered speed confidently and was gone. The people remaining headed briskly for the safe anonymity of the outside dark.

"You all right miss?"

Laura turned to find an elderly

railwayman regarding her with some concern.

"Yes thank you, quite all right."

He nodded, not convinced.

"Nothing else through here tonight miss. Not till the goods at half-past four."

His concern was genuine, and she smiled to dispel his fears.

"I've just come off the London train," she assured him. "Someone will be coming to fetch me."

"I see. Well look, I'm sorry miss, but we have to lock up now. I'm afraid you'll have to wait outside. Very sorry and all that."

She felt disappointment. It seemed to have been somebody's idea of a joke after all.

"Of course, I understand. Can you tell me, I mean I'm sure my friend will turn up, but just in case anything goes wrong, is there a hotel close by?"

He scratched his chin, thinking.

"Only one open this time of night. Not a very big town, you know. Straight across the Square. Called the Dolphin.

7

You'll have to bang a few times, I 'spect, but there's a chap on duty all night, once you can wake him up."

"Thank you."

She surrendered half her ticket and went outside the station. She was standing in what must be the Square, because she could make out the Dolphin Hotel in the faint light, directly opposite. Hoping the old man hadn't been too optimistic, she stepped briskly forward. She was almost at the corner when dipped headlights appeared, and a long black limousine swung smoothly round and towards her. Caught in the powerful beam, she blinked and waited for her eye pupils to contract. To her surprise the car stopped a few feet in front of her. Laura was puzzled but not greatly concerned. If this was some hopeful lecher looking for a stranded girl, he would be well advised to drive on. She walked purposefully on, and as she reached the driver's door it opened, and a man stepped out. He wore a dark uniform and a peaked cap, which was a hopeful sign.

"Mrs. Kilburn?"

Laura had to stop because he was right in front of her. In any case, the use of her name told her the journey had not been in vain.

"Yes. Who are you?"

"I was sent to meet you, madam. The train was a few minutes early tonight. Will you come along with me, please?"

Anticipating acceptance, he stepped back and held open the rear door.

"Just a moment. Where are we going?"

"No distance madam. We shall be there in less than half an hour."

Laura shook her head.

"I shall want to know more than that," she told him firmly. "Exactly where are we going, and exactly whom I am going to see at the other end?"

The chauffeur bowed slightly, and she wished she could see more of his face.

"I'm very sorry madam, but I am not permitted to say anything. My master says that if you are Mrs. Kilburn, and if you have come this far, then you will be willing to accompany me. He has also instructed me that if you refuse, then I am to see to it that you are

9

made comfortable at the local hotel, the Dolphin. The choice is entirely yours."

She stood in the light rain, thinking about it. The chauffeur stood by impassively, making no attempt to influence her one way or the other. Any sensible woman reasoned Laura, would fly to the Dolphin without delay. No reasonable person would even consider the alternative of driving off into the night with a total stranger to an unknown destination. But then, no sensible or reasonable woman would find themselves standing outside Pumpleigh Station at one in the morning, in response to an anonymous letter. So we'd better disregard the sensible approach, and concentrate on what you propose to do. The man who wrote the letter said he knew something about John's death. He had also hinted at a job. There were two compelling attractions there, each of them especially strong for her, for Laura Kilburn. The combination was too tailored to be accidental. The writer knew something about her, perhaps quite a lot. As to the odd business with the car, well that didn't have to be sinister. After all, she hadn't expected to be met by the mayor and the town band. On top of that, she was unusually capable of looking after herself.

"Very well."

She heard herself say it as she stepped towards the door of the car. The chauffeur straightened at once. The interior was padded leather luxury. When she was settled, the chauffeur leaned in and clicked down a small walnut table. There were two silver flasks clipped to it.

"If you would care for something to drink after the journey, madam."

"Thank you."

He withdrew and closed the door. A moment later he climbed into the front seat and the engine murmured into powerful life. Laura released one of the flasks from its clip and unscrewed the cap. The smell was decidedly familiar, but she couldn't identify it. Tilting the flask, she poured a small quantity of the liquid into the tiny cup and sipped. Of course. Daiquiri, and well iced. Now that she knew what it was, she poured herself a reasonable measure and slipped the flask back into place. Then she settled back, sipping at the drink, and running appreciative fingers along the leather seat. The car was on the outskirts of the town now, and a moment later they turned on to a four-lane highway.

"Are you completely comfortable madam?"

The sudden intrusion of the chauffeur's voice came as a mild shock. She looked quickly at the back of his head, screened from her by the thick glass partition. Microphone, of course, she reasoned.

"Yes, thank you. Very."

Oh very, very. It was warm and luxurious in the car. Somehow too, a comfort and reassurance after the uncertainty of the journey. Ridiculous. The possession of money and good taste was no pointer to the morals or motives of the possessor. Still it was nice for a change, to be riding in this superb comfort with a chauffeur in a peaked cap in the front. And drinking from a silver cup no less. Laura caught herself stifling a yawn. Good heavens, she'd be dropping off in a minute. That would never do. Quickly, she finished her drink, replacing the cup on the flask. Cigarette, that was the thing. She wouldn't nod off if she had a cigarette to concentrate on. Picking up her bag from the seat beside her, she fumbled with the clasp. Odd. It wasn't usually so stiff. A great wave of weariness came over her. This was nonsense. What would these people think if she just drifted off? Maddening, that clasp. If she could just light a cigarette. Light a cig —

The copper-gold hair slid sideways against the brown leather. In his rear mirror the chauffeur watched her. Then he smiled, and leaned forward flicking up a switch which plunged the rear of the car into darkness, as the miles rolled away under the cushioned tyres.

2

Laura stirred and opened her eyes. Her first thought was to hope the chauffeur hadn't noticed she'd dozed off. Then she realized she was no longer in a car. She was sitting in a Swedish chair of curved wood. Still not fully awake, she stared around her. The room was small, but elegantly furnished. On one wall hung what looked at a distance to be a Giorgione, though she couldn't be certain. Getting up from the chair, she found her legs not entirely reliable, and sat down again. How long had she been like this? A glance at her watch told her it was two-thirty, but whether that was morning or afternoon she had no idea. It was then that she realized there were no windows in the room.

A discreet tapping focused her eyes on the door in the far corner. Laura bit her lip and called:

"Come in."

The door opened at once and a woman came in carrying a tray. She was short, and rather over-plump. The dark hair and olive eyes confirmed her body's suggestion that she was from the Mediterranean.

"Perhaps some coffee, madame?" she smiled. "Also there are cigarettes in this box. The master, he says when you are quite ready to see him, please to ring the bell."

She pointed at the wall, where a tasselled silk cord dangled.

"Please, where am I? And what is all this about?"

To her surprise, Laura heard a note of anxiety creeping into her voice. After all, she hadn't the slightest reason to complain of her treatment this far. It wasn't his fault, the master's fault, if she couldn't keep awake.

"All will be explained, madame. Please, the coffee it will get cold."

And the little woman bobbed and bustled away with another quick smile.

She had placed the tray close by the chair, and the coffee certainly smelled

15

good. Laura shrugged and picked up the delicate little cup. The hot beverage tasted as good as it smelled, and after a couple of sips she leaned across and raised the lid of the sandalwood box. It was divided in the middle. There were Turkish cigarettes in the right compartment, Virginia on the left. Laura lifted out a Virginia and fondled the heavy porcelain table lighter before snapping it into life. She began to feel much better, and the questions mounted one on top of the other in her mind. Always a practical woman, she did not like questions without any prospect of an answer. The answers could only come from the man they called the master. Before ringing the bell however, there would be the small matter of her appearance. Her handbag was on the floor near her feet, and she rooted for comb and lipstick and other paraphernalia. There was a large mirror on one wall, and she found to her pleasure that her legs were prepared to support her this time. A couple of brisk minutes at the mirror and she felt ready to meet him. Even so, she drew her hand back once from the tasselled silk. Then, telling herself not to be such a fool she reached out again and gave it a firm jerk.

She watched the door, anxious not to miss the first look at her curious host. But it did not open. Instead, a yellow light flashed on above the door and a pleasant, not quite English voice spoke suddenly.

"I am about to come in Mrs. Kilburn. However, I thought it fair to warn you I shall be wearing a mask. This is not intended to distress you in any way, please believe that. It is simply that I do not wish you to see my face. I am coming now."

The voice was calm and reassuring, yet despite herself Laura found she had taken a step back. The door opened then and a man stepped through. He was tall and slender, wearing a black fisherman's jersey and black trousers. His face was almost entirely covered by a white mask, which made it difficult to guess at his age. The hair was thick and dark, and Laura found to her surprise she was not remotely nervous of him.

"Good evening Mrs. Kilburn. It is a great pleasure to make your acquaintance at last."

At last. What could he possibly mean by that?

"Good evening. I'm afraid I don't know your name."

"It is possible that you never will. However, you must have found my letter of sufficient interest to bring you here."

He made no attempt to approach her, but stood six or eight feet away. The whole thing suddenly struck her as slightly ridiculous, and she found herself suppressing a smile.

"I could hardly have refused, after what you wrote."

"Precisely. By the way, I trust you have been properly cared for?"

"Thank you, yes. May I ask you something? Is it night or day?"

"It is a little after two-thirty in the morning. Your — um — sleep was not very long. Please sit down, and let us talk."

Laura sat down in the chair she'd occupied before, and the masked man took a seat next to a small bureau, still well away from her.

"Mrs. Kilburn I am going to tell you some rather unusual things. So unusual in fact, that you may have some difficulty in believing them. However, I hope to convince you. After that I am going to offer you — um — employment. This too will be of a distinctly bizarre character, but I shall be perfectly serious. I do not ask you to make a decision now. You will have forty-eight hours in which to make up your mind. At the end of that time, if you decide that you are not interested, you will be perfectly free to say so, and there the matter will end. Is all that perfectly clear?"

Laura nodded, tapping ash carefully into the cut-glass bowl by her elbow.

"I ought to tell you I have a feeling this is some kind of hoax," she informed him coolly. "I ought also to tell you I react very badly to anything of that kind. Particularly since you have used my late husband's name."

"Good," he replied decisively. "A perfectly reasonable reaction, and indeed

19

one I have encountered before. To business. What did you really know about John Kilburn?"

She was taken aback by the question.

"Know about him?" she repeated dully. "Why, I was his wife."

"Ah yes," he agreed. "But I think there was an area of his life of which you knew nothing?"

She puzzled at that for a moment.

"I can't think what you can possibly mean," she said slowly. "We were a perfectly ordinary pair of busy people. And very happy. There wasn't any room for a secret life of any kind on the part of either one of us. We were far too taken up with one another, far too enmeshed for that sort of thing to be possible."

The masked man's voice was gentle when he spoke again.

"Think back, Mrs. Kilburn. Recall a very serious conversation you had with John a week before you were married."

She looked at him with surprise, and for the first time since arriving, she began to feel that the whole situation was something other than an involved dream.

20

"Before we were — but how could you possibly know anything about it?"

"Think," he encouraged. "Am I not right in saying that there was a certain sport John wished to continue?"

Now she remembered, and the whole conversation came back to her.

"His rock climbing? Yes, but — "

"And am I also not right in saying that you made a pact at that time? John would not interfere with your flying activities, and you would not try to prevent him going off on his rock-climbing excursions?"

"Yes absolutely," she nodded. "He had a very busy practice, and it was only right that he should be able to relax in — "

She stopped in the middle of a sentence, and stared.

"But how could you know that?"

He inclined his head in deprecatory fashion.

"There is no mystery, Mrs. Kilburn, the matter is really quite easily explained. You see, I instructed John to make that pact."

He waited for her reaction, which was

not slow in coming.

"You — ?" Laura got up from the chair and paced to the wall, running a hand across her forehead. "No, no. This is quite insane. I shall open my eyes in a moment, and none of this will have happened."

"Please, Mrs. Kilburn, won't you sit down? Let me tell you more about your husband."

Somehow, she found herself walking meekly back to the chair, and doing as she was told.

"You see it was necessary for John to be available at certain times, and equally necessary that no one should know what he was doing. Especially his wife."

"But he was climbing," she insisted. "Why I've sometimes driven up on a Sunday to be with him."

"Of course," agreed the other. "But it was always pre-arranged. It was the small touch of authenticity which lent, shall we say, credence to the rest of his absences."

Now she found bewilderment giving way to anger.

"And would you be good enough to tell me exactly what my husband was doing all those times? And what it was gave you the right to order his life? And just who — ?"

"Please, dear lady," he held up a hand. "Enough questions at one time. As to exactly what he was doing, no. I think it not likely that I shall tell you that at present. But you may take it he was working with me on what we felt to be important matters. Sufficiently important for him to be willing to deceive you, despite the very deep love he had for you."

He dropped his voice softly as he spoke the last words, and try as she might Laura could not contain the large tears which she felt welling up behind her eyes. She sniffed hurriedly, and the masked man turned his head away as she dabbed furiously with a perfumed square.

"It must have been damned important," she snapped.

"It was. Indeed, it still is. And that brings me to my other point. The work is indeed important. I feel, as do others, that it is quite vital. I would like you to become part of it."

Laura had control of herself again now.

"I'd rather hear about John first. You hinted in your letter there was something I didn't know about his death."

"Later, if I may. That will be explained when you know something of the work. Does it occur to you, as I am sure it must, that there is much injustice in the world?"

"Naturally. Any thinking person — "

"Quite. Not all these injustices are things which can be rectified overnight, and they are not therefore matters of my concern. I restrict myself to those things which something can and should be done, and where the law seems unable or unwilling to act."

Laura helped herself uncharacteristically to a second cigarette and puffed at it vigorously.

"I think I need that explained further," she prompted.

"Of course. Think of the gross wrongs in your newspaper every day. The slave trading in East Africa, the bombing of the innocent by these thugs in many a foreign country. Think of the industrial tycoons, making millions from the sale of armaments, and their necessary partners, the people who ferment the wars. The list is long. The international drug traffic, the deliberate destruction of food in order to maintain price levels. I need hardly go on. These things are as familiar to you as to me."

She had been listening keenly, and now she nodded.

"Oh yes, I'm in complete agreement. But these aren't things about which ordinary people can do anything. Just how do you propose setting about them?"

He chuckled, a rich pleasant sound.

"I have been, as you put it, setting about them for a long time past. So have others. John was one of them. And we are not exactly what you would describe as ordinary people. It is true that our efforts are small, as indeed they must be. But they are tangible. Do I retain your interest?"

Laura was silent for a moment.

"You say John was one of you? What could he do in the little spare time he had?"

The man waved a hand admonishingly.

"He could and did contribute most valuably. Sometimes our people get hurt. You see, not everyone approves of our efforts, and so there are casualties. John was a fine doctor, and many of our people have cause to remember him gratefully. Apart from that, he was a man of great personal courage and superbly athletic. Not all his services were exclusively medical. Indeed, I have had occasion to curb his enthusiasm at times, for his personal safety."

Yes, she thought, that would be John. She recalled one time when he had dangled precariously over a cliff to rescue a mewing kitten. At the recollection, quick tears stung again behind her eyes.

"You must forgive me," she said quickly. "All this takes time to assimilate. And yet, I find myself believing you."

He inclined the dark head in acknowledgement.

"Then we make progress. And I

fully understand your reservations. Many people have had similar doubts in the past."

"But tell me, could I know about John now?"

The man took a heavy gold cigar case in his hands and carefully removed a thick brown tube, rolling it between his fingers.

"First, tell me this. It sounds an odd question, but I am entirely serious. Would you be willing to do something for John? Something risky, possibly even dangerous. Something, I must tell you, certainly illegal."

She stared at him, puzzled.

"For John? I don't see how — But you obviously have a reason for asking. So of course the answer is yes. I would always do anything for him, now as much as ever."

He was lighting the cigar, applying flame carefully to ensure an even glow at the tip. The rich smoke drifted lazily across to where Laura was sitting.

"Then I think I may tell you about the circumstances of his death. I am afraid you must be prepared for a shock, Mrs. Kilburn. Your husband was murdered."

She sat bolt upright, disbelief quick on her face.

"No, no," she denied. "It was a car crash. A tyre must have exploded or the steering failed. Nobody could be quite certain what happened. But he veered off the road and down the side of a mountain, and was killed."

Her voice tailed away as she watched the slow shaking of the dark head.

"No. I am sorry. As you say, nobody could be quite certain what happened. That is to say, nobody who was called in after the event, and had only the wrecked car to work from. You saw the photographs. From that kind of damage not even a genius could have deduced the truth."

"And yet you know all about it."

The biting words were out before she could stop them.

"You are incredulous. I do not blame you. But I hope to convince you. John had been to France with some others — "

"He had been on Ben Nevis," she

interrupted. "I had a card — "

"He had sent you a card from Ben Nevis," continued the man inexorably. "He wrote it a week earlier, and it hardly called for great planning to arrange the date of its posting. No, he was in France. There were some people there whose business interests we were concerned with. They are — or were — engaged in smuggling arms into the Middle East. We thought we should interfere, and we did with some success. Unfortunately John and another man were followed back to this country. The first opportunity the opposition had to take their revenge occurred on that mountain road. They came from behind in another car. My people had no thought of danger. The other car overtook and simply forced John off the road. He was driving of course, and it was all as simple as that."

She sat shaking her head furiously. She didn't want to believe it. All these months she had been adjusting her mind gradually to the awful accident which had taken John away. Now, to be told it was no accident, that he hadn't needed to die at all, this was unacceptable.

"But he was alone in the car," she muttered, half to herself.

"When found, yes. But at the time it happened, no. And this is what leads me to the second reason for my asking you here."

"Please," she said wearily. "I don't think I can take very much more."

"Nevertheless, I think you would wish me to continue. Yes, there was another man in the car. As they went over the mountain side, the car hit a large piece of rock and the passenger door flew open. This other man was thrown clear, and apart from a few bruises he was unharmed."

Why, she thought bitterly. Why should he be saved and not John.

"He scrambled back to the roadway, just in time to see the other car coming back. He had to hide quickly as it stopped, and the two men inside came to look down at the wreck. He saw their faces, and he knew them."

"Then why didn't he go to the police?" demanded Laura. "If it happened as you

30

say, it was a clear case of premeditated murder."

"Alas, no," regretted the other. "It could too easily be called an accident. It is an unfortunate truth that these things happen all too often on today's roads. They may have been charged with dangerous or reckless driving. At the most they might have seen the inside of a prison for perhaps a year. That would not have been a satisfactory end to the matter. Apart from which, my people do not deal very much with the authorities. We have our own ways."

Still she could not refrain from shaking her head.

"I'm afraid I don't think much of your ways if they involve letting murderers go free."

"Please, Mrs. Kilburn, hear me out. As I said, the man who escaped with his life recognized the assassins. One was an Englishman, the other French. He could do nothing at the time, because apart from being severely shaken by the crash, he was unarmed. So he made his way back to report to me. My decision,

31

naturally, was that these two should be executed."

Despite the matter of fact way in which the statement was delivered, Laura felt a cold shiver down her back. At the same instant, she recognized in her innermost mind that her reaction was less that of shocked affront than pleasurable satisfaction. In abstract, she would have recoiled in horror from such a cold-blooded announcement, and it was a revelation to find how thin was the veneer of civilization when it came to a question of revenge for her murdered husband. The effect of his words was not lost on the watching man.

"Naturally, these things have to be arranged. They take time, money, patience. The Englishman was the better prospect, but it took us three months to find him and — er — do what was necessary."

"What happened to him?"

She blurted out the eager question, and her eyes shone. Behind the mask her host seemed to smile.

"He was an amateur yachtsman. Sailing a twelve footer off the Isle of Wight when the boat capsized on him. Most regrettable."

"Most."

And Laura relished the word and the thought.

"The other man, the Frenchman, proved even more elusive. In fact we only managed to locate him a month ago. Even then, he spotted our man and was about to take flight. We couldn't risk losing him, of course, and so we had to make last-minute improvisations, a thing I detest in our work. It too frequently leads to bungling, and in the event that is what happened on this occasion. Our — er — representative was caught by the police."

"Please tell me what happened."

"Very well. This Frenchman, whose name incidentally was Sacha Leroux — "

— Laura spotted the use of the past tense as applied to Leroux and again felt that inward satisfaction —

" — had been travelling a great deal, but his travels brought him to Trois Bains, a fishing village in a bay about forty kilometres from Marseilles. That was where we caught up with him. There was a boat leaving on the evening tide for Algiers, a smuggling matter. Leroux was not originally intending to sail with her, but he must have had word about our man, and made a quick change of plan. There wasn't time to think properly, no time for reinforcements or calculated action. The best our man could contrive was a drunken brawl outside a wharfside café, with the result that Leroux was stabbed. As I said before, our man was unable to escape arrest. You may have read something of it in the newspapers."

She thought quickly, and seemed somehow to recall a case of the kind, but could not bring it to the forefront of her mind.

"I seem to remember something."

"Clearly you would have no occasion to take an especial interest. The fact is, he is unmistakably guilty and the local prefect had no hesitation in locking him up. Equally certain is that when he goes to trial in Marseilles, which is inevitable, he will face the guillotine. That I cannot permit. And that is the reason you are here."

There was no keeping the mystification from her voice as she said:

"But I don't see what I — "

"Please. I will make it clear. You are, I know, an expert pilot."

"Yes, pretty good."

"You have also flown helicopters."

"A few times. I wouldn't call myself an expert on those."

There was an inch and a half of silver ash at the end of the cigar. Gently the masked man tipped it into an ashtray.

"This man is held in the local jail. It is a small place, and in the ordinary way, two of my people could get him out without difficulty. Unfortunately the — um — opposition have planted the thought that a break-out may be attempted, and so there are four armed men inside the jailhouse at all times. It is all very difficult. You see, although I have to secure his release, I cannot risk injury to any of the gendarmes who are only honest men protecting their community."

He paused, but if for effect it was

unnecessary. Laura Kilburn was sitting on the edge of her chair.

"So what have you worked out?" she asked.

"Stealth is regrettably ruled out. So, too, is a frontal assault. People would be hurt. The problem is clear, it is one of immobilizing the gendarmes. This will be achieved quite simply by locking them inside the jail. The cell door is solid, and my man will jam it from his side. A helicopter will drop a line with a grab fixed to it. My man will guide this through the bars of the cell, which will then be pulled out. The prisoner will climb through, and be pulled up by the helicopter. No one will be injured, no one can follow. It is that simple."

He looked at Laura, and sat waiting. She was breathing more quickly than normal, and the green eyes were shining again.

"And I will fly the helicopter?"

"If you can be persuaded," he nodded.

"H'm."

She relaxed back into the chair. This was undoubtedly the most bizarre conversation she had ever had in her life, or ever would have. One startling statement had been piled on top of another, to a point where any disbelief or critical assessment was virtually suspended. Her immediate inclination was to leap up and say 'count on me', but her head was too wise for that, judgement too balanced.

"I'm sorry," she apologized. "But I've had rather too much to take in too quickly. May I have time to think? Say half an hour?"

He rose at once, half-bowing.

"But of course. I will return in thirty minutes. Perhaps more coffee?"

"Thank you, no. I'll just sit here and think."

When he had left the room, she brought her mind to bear on the task of getting the thing into perspective.

She was Laura Kilburn, age twenty-five, newly widowed. Her love of flying and the need to communicate this to others had reawakened her old school magazine instincts to write. The first book had not been a great success, but the second, *Tall in the Sky*, had been a best-seller bringing with it the Adventure Club Annual Award. Now she produced a book per year with enough income to ensure a high living standard, and enough prestige to satisfy her moderate ego. Any onlooker, having made due allowance for her loss of John, might reasonably envy her freedom of action, her independence. Might admire her luxury flat, her small but excellent stock of wines, her famous collection of jazz piano recordings — the BBC had borrowed vintage items from her on more than one occasion. The onlooker might be forgiven for not penetrating the outer defences, because Laura did not intend that these be penetrated. No one knew the hours spent sitting by the window, staring out at the world where other people were busy with the process of living, a process which seemed no longer to have any need of Laura Kilburn. No one knew of the staring, sleepless nights, and the heavy, dragging mornings.

And now here was this man, with his crazy proposition. Her mind worried at it, picked it up, examined it from all sides. Her reason quickly produced an unanswerable indictment against such a ridiculous idea. But while her mind listened carefully to reason's arguments, weighing each one and agreeing, her heart was not paying the slightest attention. Her heart was already up in that swaying helicopter, bumping with excitement, and eager for a look at this man who had avenged John's death, had done what she would have wanted to do had she known the circumstances. A light flashed in the room, and she looked up with a start, to realize it was the light above the door again.

"I am coming in again, Mrs. Kilburn."

But that couldn't have been half an hour she thought quickly. More like five minutes. A glance at her watch told her differently. The man in the mask did not miss the movement.

"I am perhaps too soon. If you would like longer to consider? After all, I did promise you forty-eight hours."

She shook her head rapidly.

"No, no thank you. But I would like

to ask you one or two questions."

"By all means," he acknowledged courteously. "However you must be prepared for me to decline to answer."

"That's fair enough. First of all, you seem to be taking an awful chance bringing me here like this. Supposing I went to the police."

He chuckled, that rich pleasant sound she'd enjoyed before.

"To tell them what? Policemen are rational, sensible people. What kind of story would you tell them, Mrs. Kilburn?"

"Why, all of it, naturally."

"Quite. Now, think what all of it consists of. You came in response to an anonymous letter, which you have somehow lost."

Her hand moved automatically to the handbag, but stopped. She knew the letter would no longer be there.

"And where did you come? You have no idea where you are. To whom did you speak? A dark-haired man in a mask. Think of it, a mask. At three in the morning. And what did you speak of? Your husband's murder, already pronounced by a highly respected coroner as an accident. Can you not imagine the police reaction to such a story? And when you go on from there to the rest of it, you can see how improbable, not to say impossible, the whole thing is."

He was right, and she had known it before asking.

"Perhaps," she conceded. "If I were to agree, how would this operation be financed? This sort of thing costs money."

"Indeed it does. Fortunately, I am myself a wealthy man, and there are others like me who consider our work worthwhile. Later perhaps, you will learn more of our financial arrangements."

"H'm. Now as to myself. I can't just go roaming round the world at will. I am independent, as you undoubtedly know, but I do have to have some kind of explanation for publishers, a few friends, certain commitments."

"I had considered that. You have provided the solution to that problem by your knowledge of wines. A letter will be delivered at your home tomorrow. It is from the House of Charpentier in Bordeaux. They offer you a commission on any interesting local wines you encounter during any travelling you might undertake."

"But I'm not good enough," she protested. "There are many others with far deeper knowledge than mine."

"Possibly. But they do not have this independence of movement which you have, to go abroad whenever you wish. And I think you are too modest, Mrs. Kilburn. After all, if Charpentier have decided you are capable of this research, who are we to argue? You are now, in the eyes of the trade and public alike, an expert."

She smiled faintly at the implied irony, and gave up. There were many other questions she had intended to ask, but they would have to wait now.

"Very well, I accept."

"The work with Charpentiers, or my — er — proposal?"

"Both."

"Excellent. And now, it is late. I am

most anxious that the expedition begin as soon as possible. Is there any strong reason why you should go home, Mrs. Kilburn?"

"Er, why no. Nothing really. I haven't any clothes of course."

"That will be seen to."

"And, oh silly things like milk and newspapers, they'll be piling up."

"They will be cancelled."

She stood up from the chair, and smiled.

"Then I guess you have a recruit."

3

Somewhere there was a banging noise. Laura could hear it muffled through a sleep haze, and wished crossly it would go away. Instead it grew louder, and she realized suddenly there was someone knocking at the door. Sleep fell away instantly, at the memory of where she was.

"Come in," she called.

The door opened, and the little dark woman of the night before came in with a tray.

"It is lovely day, no?" she greeted.

"H'm."

Laura looked at the sun streaming through the opaque window. Yes, she decided, it was a lovely day. Whatever crazy thing she had involved herself in was going to start today. There was nothing crazy about the silver tray which was set before her.

"Thank you."

44

The smiling woman bobbed with pleasure.

"If you will wish me some more, please to push."

She pointed to the bell behind Laura's head on the wall.

"Thank you again."

Another bob, and the little woman bustled away. Laura poured coffee and looked at her watch. It was a quarter to eight, and she had been asleep four hours. It had been a long time since she had slept so quickly, so completely. Already she felt a new woman. Indeed, there was little doubt she was a new woman, she reflected. Laura Kilburn, the well-known jail-breaker. Smiling to herself, she lifted a silver cover and inspected the crisp bacon with relish. As she helped herself, and buttered a slice of toast, she noted how the new criminal Kilburn tucked into her food. The old one seldom needed anything more than a biscuit.

Ten minutes later, having eaten her biggest breakfast in months, she rested her head against the propped-up pillows and exhaled gratefully from the first

45

cigarette, the best cigarette, of the day. The white telephone on the bedside table rang, disturbing her reverie. She picked it up.

"Mrs. Kilburn, good morning."

It was a man's voice, a strange man.

"Good morning."

She didn't bother to ask who it was. Already the unusual was becoming acceptable as commonplace.

"I trust you slept well," continued the man. "You will find certain — um — garments in the wardrobe. If you will be kind enough to wear them, I will call for you in, shall we say twenty minutes?"

Twenty minutes. It looked as though her leisurely breakfast was ended.

"All right, I'll be ready."

"Thank you."

The man rang off and she replaced the receiver. She'd been idly promising herself a bath in the elegant little bathroom which led off from the bedroom. Now it looked like being a quick wash and brush up. With a final reluctant stretch she swung her feet down off the bed and crossed to the wardrobe. Opening it she found her own clothes neatly hung where she'd left them. But last night the wardrobe had otherwise been empty. Now there were three black zip-up boiler suits hanging beside her clothes. She fingered the material, which seemed to be some kind of reinforced nylon, possibly waterproof. She felt slightly disappointed. Everything else in the place was so luxurious she'd half-expected Dior or Balmain at least. In the bathroom she gave a last regretful look at the bath, then busied herself with morning preparations. Ten minutes later she had put on the first boiler suit, found it surprisingly comfortable, and smooth against the skin.

Too comfortable, she decided, looking in the long mirror. Her hips were not causing her *that* much concern. Quickly, she slipped out of the suit and tried the second one. Ah, yes. This one could have been tailored for her. It was positively flattering, in fact. She walked round, getting accustomed to the feel of the one piece suit, and to her new, semi-military appearance.

The tap at the door came quicker than expected. She crossed to open the door, and found herself looking up at a large blond-haired man, of about her own age. He smiled and inclined his head.

"How do you do, Mrs. Kilburn. I am Sven."

She took the extended hand and shook it. Sven was wearing a suit identical to her own.

"How do you do," she acknowledged. "What happens now?"

"If you are ready, please come with me."

She stepped out into the corridor and walked along beside him. He was rather good-looking she decided. He certainly looked Nordic enough to justify his name. But something told her that questions were not a part of the social programme. Together they went down a narrow stairway, through a door at the bottom. They crossed a small hall, went through another door, then more steps downwards. The absence of windows made it difficult to judge, but she guessed they must by now be well under the house.

At the bottom stood another man, dressed as they were.

"Mrs. Kilburn, this is George."

She shook hands with George, a short, plumpish man of about fifty.

"A thirty-two wasn't it?" queried George.

Laura looked at Sven for guidance. He saw her puzzlement and grinned quickly.

"Yes, I would think so."

George took a bunch of keys from his pocket and opened a set of double doors. Inside was a steel grille, for which he had another key ready. Laura watched with wide open eyes as the grille slid aside to reveal rows of revolvers and automatic pistols. Sven looked at her with amusement.

"Are you at all familiar with weapons, Mrs. Kilburn?"

"Why er, no," she stammered. "That is, I used to be pretty good with a longbow, but I imagine that hardly qualifies."

Even the solemn George managed a

fleeting smile at that.

"Well no, Mrs. Kilburn," he said regretfully. "I'm afraid it isn't quite the same thing. Take this for instance."

Reaching inside he lifted out a black automatic, hefted it in his palm with evident affection, and handed it to her.

"A beautiful piece of machinery," he said feelingly. "That is a Smith and Wesson .32 eight shot automatic, and as fine a piece of tooling as you'll find in the trade."

She took it nervously. The weapon was cold in her hand, but not as heavy as she'd expected. It smelled faintly of oil.

"Please sign here."

George produced a bound register from the cupboard. There was an entry all made out to Mrs. L. Kilburn, and all it required was her signature. He had a pen waiting too.

"Does this mean I have to keep it?"

Laura did not relish the idea, and her tone indicated the fact.

"Not in the technical sense, no," explained George. "Normally, unless you're down here and you happen to want it, or else it's been issued to you for a cruise, then it remains locked up with me. That signature means it is your personal weapon, and it won't be made available to anyone else."

"Oh, I see."

She didn't, she told herself, scribbling quickly. She didn't see at all. And what on earth did he mean, issued to me for a cruise?

"It's rather pointless, I'm afraid. You see, I don't even know how to shoot the thing."

"That will be remedied, Mrs. Kilburn, as soon as you are ready."

Sven took her arm and pointed along the corridor.

"Oh."

Clutching the gun tight she walked in the direction indicated. Sven held out a hand to George who lifted another weapon from the rack and passed it to him.

"In here."

Sven opened a door, and they stepped into a long low room. No, thought Laura, not a room, not a real room. It was very narrow and bare of furniture. The far end was in darkness, and they were standing before a kind of counter. There were small cardboard boxes stacked to one side. Sven opened one of the boxes.

"Watch me please."

She watched curiously as he appeared to slip out the butt of the gun in his hand. No, it wasn't the butt, it was a kind of inner case.

"Clip," he explained, holding it for her to see.

"Oh," she nodded.

She said 'oh' several times in the next few minutes, while Sven ran her through the drill of ejecting the clip and reloading. Finally she thought she had it right.

"How are your eyes?" he queried.

"Pretty good, thanks. I haven't got round to needing glasses yet."

"Fine."

He pressed a switch on the wall, and the far end of the room glowed suddenly. Laura could make out round targets.

"First we practise how to aim. Hold the gun up so, and please keep your finger away from that trigger."

She followed his movements carefully.

"You bring the gun down slowly, aiming for the centre of the target. The one on the left will be yours. Like this."

Again she copied exactly what he did.

"Good. Now it is time to shoot. You see this small catch on the side? This is the safety. As it is, it has the gun out of action. Once you push it sideways like this — " the catch clicked gently " — then the gun is ready."

Feeling unaccountably nervous, Laura pushed slightly against the catch. The lesson continued, Sven explaining again and again the rudiments of aiming the weapon. She wished he'd get on with it. Having got this far, she at least wanted to shoot the thing.

"That will do I think," he told her finally. "There is one last thing I have to tell you. Ammunition is expensive. As the ability to shoot well is primarily for one's own protection, we do not supply ammunition free for target practice. As a newcomer, you are allowed three clips free of charge. That is to say, twenty-four shots."

"That sounds quite a lot," she replied.
Sven grinned. He had nice teeth.

"It sounds a lot, Mrs. Kilburn. However, if you should become a trifle gun-happy, you will find that three clips have gone before you realize it."

"That's not likely to happen. Tell me, suppose I use them all, what is the next stage?"

"Then you pay. The charges are most reasonable. The cost is one shilling per shot."

"That sounds reasonable, but — "

He held up a hand, and she stopped in mid-sentence.

"Please, there is more. That is the basic charge. Provided you have a bull or an inner only. Either of the outer rings puts up the cost to five shillings per shot. If you aim off the target altogether, it will be ten shillings."

"I see. One had better be good then."

"Very good," he agreed. "Or very rich. Now, we fire. Together."

She raised the gun again, bringing it down slowly towards the target. As the sights aligned she pulled her hand tight.

The bang was louder than expected and the weapon bucked in her hand like a shying horse. The target was unmarked.

"Too quick, too convulsive. The pressure must be even and firm. Again."

She fired again, better this time, but still at little risk to the target. With the fourth shot she clipped the top right hand corner. The fifth and sixth landed close to it.

"High right," muttered Sven.

"I'm sure I aimed the last one straight," she protested.

"Possibly. Some weapons have their own characteristics. It is only by using them one learns what these are. Yours seems to have a tendency to fire high and to the right. The remedy is to aim slightly below and to the left of the target. You will try please."

She did this, and was rewarded with one complete miss and one at the left hand edge. Then the gun clicked on her next try.

"It is empty, Mrs. Kilburn," said the blond man.

"Empty? But it can't be. Why I've only — "

She stopped talking as he nodded knowingly. Slightly irritated with herself, she slipped out the clip and reloaded. At the second loading, she slowly grew to learn the weapon, scoring two outers and one glorious inner. When she made to reload again, Sven held out a hand.

"Not now. You have done enough. Believe me, you will be glad of that third clip to accustom yourself once more to the feel of the weapon next time you come here."

Disappointed, and with one last triumphant look at the solitary precious inner, she followed him out of the room. At the end of the passage, George waited. He took the guns, and at once set about cleaning them.

"George is one of our secret weapons," explained Sven. "It would be hard to find another arsenal where the stock is kept in such prime condition."

George acknowledged the tribute with a quick nod of his head, but Laura could tell he was pleased.

"Thank you George," she added.

Sven led her back up the stairs, and into the hallway at the top. Instead of crossing it to the other staircase, he moved off to the left, Laura hurrying along beside him.

"Tell me, are there many people here?" she wondered.

Sven looked at her direct, and this time there was no smile.

"Mrs. Kilburn, I must beg you not to ask questions. We do not know you yet, not at all. And curiosity about our — um — activities is a most undesirable quality in anyone. Especially so with an untried member like yourself. This way, please."

Chastened, she subsided into silence as they walked along. They seemed to be in the hall of a large country house, but as there were no windows, the effect was more that of a display room in a museum.

"Please."

Sven stopped before a doorway and pushed what she had assumed to be a light switch. At once there was a humming beyond the door which told her it was a lift. The noise stopped and Sven opened the door, motioning her inside. He followed her and closed the door, pressing a button. There was no sensation of movement.

"You have flown a helicopter before?"

"Yes, just a little."

"What type, please?"

"A Sikorsky Six. Why?"

He nodded, searching his memory.

"Ah yes, this is the military version, a large one I think?"

"Large enough," she agreed.

"You are not then familiar with the Rondo."

"Rondo?" She was as puzzled as she sounded. "I don't think I've ever heard of it. Is it a new type?"

"Quite new. It is manufactured in Brazil, by quite a small company. It is also quite a small machine, which has certain advantages."

He didn't offer to explain what the advantages were, and she didn't dare to ask. A moment later he leaned forward and opened the door. Laura had not

58

realized the lift had stopped. Stepping out she found herself standing in bright sunshine. After the continual artificial light of the building she had to blink rapidly, adjusting her eyes. Turning, she saw that Sven was having the same trouble.

"Bright, isn't it?"

"It certainly is," he nodded.

They were on the top of the building, standing in a little well surrounded by high walls. On her right was a steel door, and her escort now produced a key. The door swung smoothly open.

"Wow!"

It wasn't her most elegant expression, but Laura could not withhold it. They emerged on to a roof garden, but not like any she'd ever seen before. This was no elaborate arrangement of boxes and flower pots, but literally a garden in the sky. Everywhere was a riot of colour, and there were even two greenhouses at the far end. Not that she noticed those immediately, because on the twenty-foot square of lawn in the middle of the roof stood a small black helicopter

"What a beauty," she muttered, half to herself.

"I thought you would like it," Sven replied. "I think you will find it just as interesting inside as out. Come."

She walked beside him towards the machine. It bore no marks of any kind, no numbers, no insignia. No wonder there was a six-foot parapet all around the roof. This was a private landing field.

Sven slid back the cockpit door and she climbed in. At once, her practised eye took in the elegance of the fittings, the shine of the instruments. This machine had been tended with loving care. She sat in the pilot's seat, noting the panel layout, which had been designed for maximum efficiency and minimum inconvenience.

"Can you fly it?" demanded Sven.

She had almost forgotten there was someone with her, and the sound of his voice startled her slightly.

"I think so. Given a little time."

"You have it, Mrs. Kilburn. I am to leave you here to familiarize yourself with the machine. You will have two hours. Two things to note please. You are not to attempt to fly it, not even run the engine. Secondly, you are not, absolutely not, to attempt to look over the wall."

"Why should I want to?"

"You will hear me please."

And there was that in his voice which told Laura it would be an extremely bad idea to look over the wall.

"I hear you."

"Mrs. Kilburn, it is to be hoped you will use the time well. There is a good possibility you will fly her tonight."

"Without any practice?" she protested.

"You will be permitted one hour for practice. My information is that you are a most skilled pilot. Surely once you know your controls, your instruments, the rest is plain sailing?"

"Well, I certainly hope so."

He gave one of his brief nods, and walked away. She sat there musing for a few moments, then looked at her watch. Already five minutes of her two precious hours had ticked away, and she was going to need every minute. Determinedly, she concentrated her attention on the job in hand, excluding all thoughts about her strange situation. The instruments were all familiar enough, it was more a matter of memorizing the layout than learning anything new. Except that stabiliser control, she hadn't seen one quite like that before. And so she became gradually immersed in what she was doing.

She was busy inspecting the hydraulic jacks on the port leg when she became aware of someone approaching. Looking up she saw Sven. A quick time check told her the two hours were up.

"So soon?"

"I regret, yes. You have seen enough?"

"Enough to make me confident to try flying her. What time will that be?"

"As soon as it is dark. Let us say, eight o'clock."

"Good. Well perhaps I could have another session up here this afternoon?"

"I am afraid that will not be possible. Other arrangements have been made. And now if you are ready, it is time for lunch."

As they walked back towards the metal door, Laura said:

"The chopper will carry only four

people and supplies. We might squeeze in a fifth person without supplies, but he wouldn't be very comfortable. Always supposing I don't have to carry extra fuel."

"Everything will be attended to, at the proper time."

They rode down in the lift, but not to the hall. This time when it stopped she was in a corridor that seemed somehow familiar. Of course, it was the far end of the corridor containing the room where she had slept the night before. Sven led her back to what she instinctively thought of as her own door.

"Please, lunch will be brought here to you," he explained.

She was disappointed. Instead of meeting some of the others, assuming there were others, she was to be isolated again. But she smiled cheerfully.

"And then what?"

"I do not know," he said frankly. "You will be told. Goodbye for now."

And she was alone in the room. There were one or two oil marks on her hands and she was in the process of washing these off when there was a knock at the outer door.

"Come in," she sang.

It was the bobbing maid again. This time she carried an even larger tray than at breakfast. She set the tray down on a small table, and fussed around setting out the dishes. Laura's nose wrinkled appreciatively.

"Please, you eat now."

Laura sat down. The food was plain, but good. Pork chop, new potatoes, a cob of corn. There was blackcurrant tart and fresh cream under the other cover. She set to work busily, and to her surprise, ate everything in sight. When she had finished, she leaned back contentedly, exhaling a lazy stream of smoke. Not for the first time, she realized how relaxed she felt in this extraordinary place. After all, she reasoned, a girl is not required to shoot off guns and fly helicopters from rooftops every day in the week. And yet she seemed to be accepting it all as quite natural. It was because of John of course. Clever devil, that man in the mask. He'd known the key to

64

Laura Kilburn, that one. If there was something, anything, she could do to fill that awful gap, especially something that might somehow help John, wherever he was, then she must do it.

Well, no one seemed to be in a hurry to fetch her. It wouldn't hurt if she just lay back on the pillow for a few minutes. Crushing the cigarette, she slipped off her shoes and sank on to the bed. Just for a minute, mind. They knew where to find her when they —

4

The telephone jangled, and Laura woke with a start. The room was in darkness. Groping for the phone she said sleepily: "M'm?"

"Time to be ready, Mrs. Kilburn." It was the voice of the masked man. "Shall we say ten minutes?"

"M'm. I mean yes."

She found the light switch and looked at her watch. Seven-forty. Good heavens, she'd been asleep six hours. No, that couldn't be. She hadn't been that tired. Then her eyes went to the small table, now clear of dishes. They couldn't have drugged her, surely? They wouldn't do that, there was no need. Still, she *had* been asleep all that time.

No time to think about it now. Must hurry and get ready. Ready for what? She hadn't the faintest idea. She seemed to be forever hurrying around getting prepared for callers, with no indication of

66

what they were calling about. Presumably she was to try flying the chopper now. Then what?

There was a knock at the door. It was Sven again.

"Did you sleep well?"

"How did you know I — oh, never mind. I'm all set."

Looking quickly around to make sure she'd left nothing, her eyes fell on her handbag. Surely she wouldn't need that?

"I suppose I won't need the handbag?" she asked. Sven hesitated.

"Well — er — I always think a lady looks properly dressed if she carries one with her."

An answer and no answer. She picked up the bag and slung it on her arm.

"Is that better?"

For a moment his impassive mask slipped a little.

"You are very attractive," he acknowledged. "Shall we go?"

And thank you kindly sir, she thought. It was nice to know the man was human, anyway.

They went up in the lift. On the roof,

a light breeze was blowing, and there was a half moon. Laura breathed in deeply.

"What a wonderful night."

"Yes."

In the helicopter, the cabin lights were on, but there was no other illumination up there other than the moonlight. She climbed inside, realizing at once the value of the time she'd spent that morning. The cabin interior was like an old friend, everything familiar.

"We begin," said Sven. "When you are quite ready, please switch off all lights except the instrument panel. Then take her up a few feet and manoeuvre around."

"Right. For how long?"

"Till you are satisfied you have complete control."

"Very well. Are you coming up with me?"

"No. I am to observe from the ground. If you get into any kind of difficulty, you are to come down at once. And just a few feet please to begin. Say four or five."

She gave him a half-salute, and switched off the interior lights. A final check round of the instruments and she was ready to start. The engine sprang instantly to life, and she patted the control column affectionately.

"Not just a pretty face, are you my beauty."

Gently, she applied pressure and with a smooth motion the machine left the ground. Or rather, the roof. This was going to be a pleasure, she told herself.

Leaning against the parapet wall, Sven watched as the helicopter went through its paces. He was not able to fly it himself, but he'd had plenty of opportunity as a passenger to know when the machine was being flown and when it was merely being operated. This girl was good, he could see that. And somehow, he was pleased about it. He let her stay up about twenty minutes, enough to satisfy both of them that she knew what she was about. Excellent.

He ground out his cigarette carefully and walked across to stand in front of the helicopter where Laura would be able to see him. Then he waved for her to come down. He had to make the movement several times before she saw him. At once, the big bird settled easily down on the turf.

Laura switched off, gave the control column a final pat, and jumped down to the ground.

"She's lovely. I was dying to take her off somewhere and have a real jaunt. I suppose that isn't possible?"

"We will see. Come, there is someone waiting to talk to you."

Slightly deflated by his apparent lack of enthusiasm, she stood quietly beside him in the lift. This time they emerged into the big hall again and Sven led her to a pair of double doors. These he opened, and they went through, the doors closing silently behind them.

There were two men in the room, the man in the mask and another one, Japanese looking. She hadn't seen him before. They were looking at some papers on a desk. The man in the mask spoke first.

"Ah Mrs. Kilburn, good evening."

"Good evening."

She looked expectantly at the oriental

who was making no bones about inspecting her closely. The man in the mask looked at Sven who nodded positively.

"Good. Will you both look at this please."

They went to join the others at the desk. Spread out on it was a large scale contour map and on top of that a large sketch.

"This is an accurate sketch of the village," explained the Japanese. To Laura's astonishment he had a pronounced North American accent. "As you see, it is not a big place. Most of the life centres around the harbour. There has been a tendency since the last war, for people to build their homes further back from the sea, and that accounts for this ribbon development out this direction. Seafarers long ago called it the Place of the Two Hills. The reason isn't far to seek."

He moved the sketch to one side and they looked at the map beneath. A square of magnifying glass lay over the section of coastline they were interested in. A quarter of a mile inland and clearly

71

marked, a gentle hill rose at either end of the village.

"To the east, that is to say on the Marseilles side," the brown finger pointed, "that hill is dominated by the new Catholic church. The old one was damaged during the war. I need hardly say what a wonderful landmark the new one makes. Here is a picture of it."

He placed on the table a coloured post card, the kind of thing filled in hurriedly by tourists passing through. The church was modern in design, and stood out starkly against the skyline. The hill was rather higher than it looked from the map.

"What is the height, please?"

Laura found herself asking before realizing it. The Japanese looked at her with approval.

"It is not very big. The hill itself, seven hundred feet, the church a further eighty. Say eight hundred feet at the highest point.

"Above sea or ground level?"

"Sea-level."

She looked at it again.

"I suppose it's too much to hope there's a navigation light up on top?"

"I regret not. Now, as you can see, the photograph does not show the hill to the west of the village. The reason is, it is no more than a hill. By comparison with the other, with this handsome church on it, the western hill looks bare. There is no place for it on a tourist picture. However, here is a recent picture, from above."

He laid a glossy photograph on top of the postcard. The second hill was indeed bare, just a few thick bushes sprouting in clumps from its sides. To the right of the picture was a low square building, standing apparently alone, and halfway down the hill.

"This is our target."

"Strange place for a jail," offered Sven. "Stuck up there."

"You have to know the history," continued their instructor. "These small harbours being what they are, there are frequent waterfront brawls, and the gendarmerie continually have to bang a few heads together and give them a night to cool off. At one time the jail was much nearer the harbour. The authorities found that if a man's crewmates decided they'd like to have him out, they were quite capable of going to the jail-house and removing him. After the place had been rebuilt half a dozen times, it was decided to shift the jail right outside the harbour area. Sailors on the spree, who were quite happy to walk a few hundred yards with a skinful of liquor, found their enthusiasm died off fast when they had to tramp clear of the town and then climb an unlit hill. The rescue attempts fell off sharply."

They all grinned at each other. Laura looked back at the photograph.

"From what angle was this shot? I mean how does it line up in relation to the post card?"

Again the Japanese's eyes gleamed appreciatively.

"They can be placed almost side by side," he explained. "That is to say, the jail is on the eastern slope of the hill, and in a line with the eastern hill." Anticipating a further question, he went on. "And the western hill is just under a thousand feet."

The masked man had been watching and listening so far, without interruption. Now he said:

"Could you locate the jail in the dark, Mrs. Kilburn? From the air."

She pouted thoughtfully, thinking about it.

"I don't know," she admitted finally. "My navigation is pretty good, but whether I can locate one small building beside one rather small hill, at eight hundred miles distance, in the dark, that's asking an awful lot."

The masked man nodded gravely.

"I would think that a fair summing-up. On the other hand, if you were only five miles away from it to begin with?"

"I could almost do it blindfold."

"We shall see. You would not object to what I believe is called a dummy run?"

"I'd welcome it."

"Then, let us proceed."

They all began to walk from the room. Laura walked with them, wondering what kind of test she had to face this time. They went back up to the roof, and all climbed into the helicopter. The Japanese handed her a piece of paper.

"Five miles from here there is a farmhouse. In between are a few small hills and a thick wood. I have given you the precise bearings from here, also wind speeds and directions as of one hour ago. Is it enough?"

"It should be," she replied doubtfully. "With the other one I would have the coast line and the lights of the village to help me of course."

"Quite. But not if you were blindfold, I imagine."

She flushed in the near darkness of the cabin.

"Very well. Please slide the door."

"It is a warm evening," said the masked man. "The fresh air will be pleasant."

Laura turned in her seat and tried to look at all three of them at the same time.

"There is one thing we have to have clear at the outset. I am in this, for better or worse. I will do as you say, and I will follow whatever plan you decide. But once we are in the air, whether in this or a proper aircraft, I am the captain. If you want a taxi-driver, employ one. Nobody is going to take away my authority as captain in the air."

The men looked at each other, and for a long moment nothing was said. Laura could sense that these three knew one another well enough for words to be unnecessary.

"Sven, you are nearest," said the masked man quietly. "I believe you heard what the pilot said."

At once Sven turned and slid the door on its smooth grooves. Laura studied the printed instructions on the paper.

Whether the others realized it or not, Laura knew this was as much a test of the instruments as of her capabilities. She would have to rely on them entirely to set her down at the right spot. Indeed, for all practical purposes she might as well have a blacked-out cabin, the way she'd had to learn back in navigation-school days. With no idea where she was to begin with, there would be no landmarks to help her, no rivers, railway lines, trunk roads. It was purely an instrument flying exercise, and all she could hope was that the instruments were up to it.

"We're off, gentlemen."

The powerful little engine ticked over at once, and she began to lift them up towards the moonlit sky. Once over the building, a quick glance at the surrounding terrain told her she'd been right. There wasn't one recognizable feature. Using the house as the centre of a circle she flew around it twice, confirming her knowledge of the controls and accustoming her eyes to the darkness outside. When she was satisfied, she set the compass, crossed her fingers, and set off. As a test, it was gruelling. The short distance permitted no time for adjustments or last-moment corrections. She had to be bang on target the first time, and her eyes flicked continually from compass to A.S.I. to clock.

"Sometime in the next twenty seconds we should be over the farmhouse," she reported. "Is it safe to go lower?"

"You are safe down to forty feet at least," replied Sven.

The nose tilted and she took the machine down. Even in the poor moonlight she ought to be able to see something as big as a farmhouse. But there was nothing below or ahead. Laura felt let down. Then a hand touched her shoulder.

"Look right."

It was the voice of the Japanese. She looked, and about a quarter of a mile away was a luminous blob.

"The farmhouse," said the masked man. "I arranged for a little paint to appear on the roof. Please take us back now."

Minutes later she was circling the house again, and dropped down in the exact centre of the little patch of turf on the roof. Switching off, she told herself she'd failed the test, and wondered what would happen next.

They all climbed out. No one said anything as they got back in the lift and went back downstairs to the room where they had studied the map. The Japanese gathered up the photographs, and slipped them into a flat leather case along with the map. The masked man lifted a telephone and said:

"Ready now, George."

Laura could not wait any longer for someone to speak to her.

"Well?" she asked. "Who will fly you now?"

They all looked at her in surprise.

"I do not understand, Mrs. Kilburn," replied the masked man. "Have you changed your mind?"

"No, of course not, but I botched it didn't I? I mean, a quarter of a mile error is pretty bad."

The Japanese laughed, and even Sven managed a smile.

"What do you mean? You did splendidly. Far better than we had hoped. The small error was nothing in the circumstances. And on the actual cruise you will have a lighted village, a coastline and a hill. My dear lady, we regard your effort as first class."

The masked man gave her a brief bow as he spoke, and the others nodded encouragingly. Laura felt herself blushing. Again he'd used that word cruise, and again she wondered at its significance. Just then the door opened, and in came the lugubrious George. In his hand he carried two black belts, and from each hung a pistol holster. He handed one to Laura and the other to the Japanese.

"Thank you George. I will see you in the morning."

It was a dismissal. George nodded and went out. The masked man turned to Sven.

"There will be nothing else now until tomorrow. Can you come and see me in control at four-thirty tomorrow morning?"

"Right." Sven looked at Laura. "Good luck to you. Both of you."

She found herself saying thank you. Until this moment, the impact of the whole operation hadn't really struck home. Now, here she was buckling on a gunbelt, and feeling slightly foolish about it. Especially as she noted the practised ease with which the Japanese had swung his around his middle. The holster felt heavy against her hip. When the door had closed behind Sven, the masked man looked at her, noting the way she fumbled with the holster.

"Now, Mrs. Kilburn, it becomes

81

necessary to tell you one or two things. As you will have gathered your companion will be this gentleman. He is Mr. Nagumi, and he has much experience of our activities. You will regard him as being in charge, and if anything should go wrong, if something does not go precisely as planned, you may have every confidence in following his instructions. Mr. Nagumi is not without some experience of last minute hitches."

It was a private joke, and Nagumi's face twitched in a quick grin. Laura had already decided from her short acquaintance with him, that the Japanese was a man who would know what to do.

"You will leave tonight. I believe you are fully rested?"

Was he being sarcastic about her sleeping that afternoon, she wondered.

"I think you probably made certain of that," she told him coolly.

"Indeed yes. I hope you did not mind, but it is quite essential that you should be absolutely alert and in trim. Now, a word about the gun. It is not for aggression, but for self-protection. The only reason you have it is in case certain friends of ours should put in an appearance. They are not expected, but they do know our man is in the jail. They will know also that it would not be our usual policy to leave him there. If they should be on the scene, you may need the gun. But now I tell you one rule which you will not break. You will never, absolutely never, use a gun against policemen or soldiers, or any other person who is only carrying out instructions and doing a job of work. For instance, this little matter tonight — "

Tonight. She was really going tonight. Laura's imagination began to race away, but she had to jerk her mind back to what was being said. She'd already missed a few words.

" — and the police are armed. This I already know. If they can get into a position to fire on you, they will do so. There will be no return fire. It is no part of our intention to shoot down innocent people. You fully understand what I am saying Mrs. Kilburn? As an organization we have few rules, very few. But the few we have are completely inviolable. This is one of the most important."

"I could never bring myself to shoot at a policeman anyway," she assured him. Or probably anybody else either, she admitted to herself privately.

"That is the answer I normally receive, at this stage. It is not quite such a simple matter, in the heat of the moment and when you are under fire."

Ridiculous, she thought to herself. He didn't know as much about Laura Kilburn as he thought, if he imagined for a moment she could ever bring herself to do such a thing.

The masked man was not looking at her now. He was turning to the table from which he picked up two envelopes.

"These are emergency money issues," he explained, handing one to each of them. "Inside you will find one hundred and fifty pounds. This is divided equally between English pounds, French francs, Spanish pesetas. There is enough to get you to a place of safety if you should run into any difficulties. None are expected, naturally. On your safe return, the money will be returned to me."

She took the thick envelope and made to put it in her left breast pocket. Nagumi said quickly:

"The other pocket please, Mrs. Kilburn."

She shrugged and unbuttoned the flap of the other pocket, slipping the envelope inside.

"Now, to business. You will leave here in fifteen minutes, and fly direct to the Bristol Channel. Nagumi knows the directions. There you will transfer to a flying boat, which will take you at once direct to a ship in the Mediterranean. The ship, and Nagumi will give you more details later, is some one hundred and ninety miles north of the island of Minorca. Your task will be based from the ship."

Again, Laura found her mind wandering. Flying boats, ships, the Mediterranean. Whatever else might be involved in this business, boredom was unlikely to loom large.

85

"You understand all that, Mrs. Kilburn?"

The question brought her attention back quickly. The man must have spotted her imaginings, she thought guiltily.

"Oh yes, thank you. Quite clear. About the Bristol Channel leg, I'm a bit worried about my knowledge of the Channel."

"There is no need. Nagumi will pilot the helicopter."

"But I thought — "

And she looked with quick irritation at Nagumi, who studiously avoided noticing. Were they making a fool of her?

"Let me explain," said the masked man. "You are required to carry out the actual operation. That is why you are here. But we do not expect you to perform miracles, Mrs. Kilburn. It is one thing, as you yourself have pointed out, to locate a moderate sized hill beyond a coastline and a lighted village, from a take-off point of five miles. It is another matter entirely to pilot a comparatively strange machine in the darkness without lights to a rendezvous in the Bristol

Channel with anything so small as a flying boat. It is no criticism of your talents. It is rather a proper regard for the security of the enterprise, for the personal safety of Nagumi and yourself, and to be quite honest, for a valuable machine."

It made sense, of course. Everything this man said made sense, once you accepted the bizarre starting point.

Mollified, she nodded.

"Then, if you are quite ready, Mrs. Kilburn?"

Nagumi looked at her expectantly.

"Yes. Yes, quite ready."

The masked man rose, holding out his hand.

"I have sent your husband on many a cruise," he told her softly. "It gives me great personal satisfaction to be sending you on one the purpose of which is to avenge his death."

She felt a quick lump in her throat, nodded briskly, and followed Nagumi out of the room.

5

In the ordinary way, Laura detested flying as a passenger. In her mind, there was only one proper place for her in any kind of flying machine, and that was behind the controls. But tonight, with her mind still in a whirl, she found herself content to sit beside Nagumi and watch. She had noted in the first few minutes his complete mastery of the little ship, and now she was able to relax slightly and even spend time peering down the fifteen hundred or so feet to the ground. It was an eerie, isolated sensation, to be cruising along without lights, and one not untinged with fear. The importance of maintaining allotted heights and flight paths had been so thoroughly instilled into her that she expected any moment to see some huge passenger liner looming up ahead. But she noted the meticulous care with which Nagumi watched the chronometer, adjusting speed, height and even occasionally course every few minutes.

'He must have every passenger flight detail memorized,' she thought.

"I see you are observing the frequency with which I adjust course and so forth," said Nagumi suddenly. It was as though he was reading her thoughts. "And, since you do not ask, I assume you have worked out for yourself that this is to avoid any possibility of contact with any passenger flights."

She looked at him oddly.

"Are you a mind-reader too?" she demanded.

He laughed lightly, watching the time.

"By no means," he assured her. "But an expert flier, like yourself, would be less than human not to observe the way someone else works. And you could scarcely fail to wonder whether I have the slightest idea what I am doing. In fact, it is one of my little tasks to keep absolutely up to date with all new routes and timings. It would not be at all in keeping with our intentions if I were to cause an accident to innocent people."

'And people who are not innocent?' wondered Laura. But she kept the question to herself, suspecting that the answer, if she received one, would not please her.

"In about twenty minutes we shall arrive," he continued. "And I think I may promise you a flying experience even you will not have encountered before."

She sat wondering what that was supposed to mean, but if he was hoping for a question she would disappoint him.

"You see a switch on your left above the door?"

She felt around with her fingers.

"I can feel it, yes."

"When I say Now, will you be good enough to flick it on instantly?"

"Of course."

To avoid any delay, she kept her fingers resting on the sliderail of the door. Nagumi stared at the clock, bringing the helicopter two degrees west.

"Now," he clipped.

She snapped down the switch, and immediately felt she was flying through

90

a green cloud. Then she realized what had happened. Green lights above and below the fuselage were throwing off a strong light.

"Look below."

She looked down and there was a big aircraft, two hundred feet below and passing away to their left. It could be a VC 10, she thought.

"It is the one dangerous moment of the flight," Nagumi went on smoothly. "Three routes almost converge at this point. I cannot avoid them all with absolute safety, so I fly as close as I dare to one of them, and put on the lights. It gives them ample opportunity to take evasive action."

"I see."

She watched the lighted ship disappear.

"But why not have ordinary lighting, surely they would see that much better?"

"They would certainly see us very much better, and that is of course to be avoided. No, the green lighting has been most effective on hundreds of occasions. You will have read about them."

Read about them. What could he

possibly mean by that?

"You do not understand? In your newspapers, Mrs. Kilburn. Tomorrow morning there will be an item on the front pages of them all. What is it they call us? Unidentified flying objects. You are sitting in one at this moment. Please switch off now."

She did so, and the darkness seemed even more impenetrable than before. Despite the circumstances, she smiled quietly to herself. A real UFO, and here she was inside it. It would explain so many things, too. She visualized the kind of reports that would be published the next day, and from serious people too. Well, she thought, I've already solved one of the great mysteries of the twentieth century, and the adventure isn't even properly under way yet. There were lights below now, dotted out in the irregular lines that denoted a coast line.

"Won't someone see us go down?" she queried.

"No," he replied. "Because we do not go down. See?"

She looked where he pointed. High up

on the instrument panel, a small red light had began to glow. Nagumi eased back on the controls, and they begun to climb. The glowing became less frequent, and Nagumi turned the nose until it became very rapid. Then, quite quickly, it was constant. The helicopter levelled out.

"There."

Dead ahead, and not more than a quarter of a mile away, the lights of a big aircraft came into view. Nagumi cut back the power until they were barely maintaining height. Above his head the small red light burned brighter.

"We'll hit it," and Laura tried to keep her voice calm.

"No," he said matter-of-factly.

She could see the ship quite clearly now, a large flying boat. It had turned and was moving away from them in the same direction. The belly of the machine was lighted up, and she watched fascinated as what seemed to be bomb doors slid open underneath. The red light was now intense in the cabin, and Nagumi gave the helicopter full throttle as they surged forward beneath the flying boat. The noise was excruciating, but Laura scarcely noticed as she stared up into the lit interior of the big ship above. Now a green light appeared suddenly beside the red. Slowly the little helicopter rose up straight into the bowels of the flying boat. Beneath them, the big doors began to close. As they locked in place, Nagumi set the helicopter down till it was resting on them. A siren sounded above the noise of the engines and Nagumi switched off. He didn't even bother to look down, she noted.

Now, everything was quiet. Laura sat, completely bewildered, and yet elated at the experience. Watching her, Nagumi said:

"I think I promised an unusual experience?"

"But what is that thing? How does it work? I mean, I can see it's some kind of homing device."

She pointed at the place where the red and green lights had been shining so brightly a few seconds before. Nagumi chuckled.

"The Z-box?" he chuckled. "Ah yes,

there are many who would be interested in that little beauty, I regret I cannot satisfy your curiosity. However, come. We must be moving."

He slid open the door on his side, looking round to see if she was doing the same. After a moment's hesitation, she did, and stepped down on to a rubberized surface. As she did so a man, a stranger, stepped into view and began to secure the helicopter into waiting metal rings. He was dressed like she was.

"Good evening," she offered tentatively, but there was no reply.

"Come, Mrs. Kilburn."

Nagumi was half-way up a metal ladder, and she followed him quickly. At the top was a small platform, and an open door leading out into a gangway. He waited for her to catch up, then walked along the narrow passageway. They passed several doors with numbers on them. Her guide paused at number eleven.

"In here, please."

He opened the door, and Laura stepped through, anxious to meet some of the people on this extraordinary craft. The little room was empty and she felt disappointment, followed quickly by alarm as the steel door shut behind her. The feeling went almost at once. After all, she reasoned, if anyone had intended her harm, they had had ample opportunity in the past twenty-four hours. It was no doubt some more of their strict security.

The room was furnished with a steel bunk attached to the wall, one chair, a small table, and was carpeted throughout. She wondered idly who had used it last, and for what purpose. Sitting down, she felt around for cigarettes and lit one. There was no window, but in any case there was nothing to see outside but the blackness of the night. After a few minutes there was a tap at the door, and Nagumi entered.

"Everything is in order," he confirmed.

She nodded, as though pleased to hear it, although without the least idea of just what was in order. Or, for that matter, what could be wrong with it if it wasn't.

"We shall be airborne for almost three

hours," he continued. "I understand you are a formidable gin rummy player, Mrs. Kilburn."

"Not me," and she was pleased they could be wrong about some things. "I hardly know the game at all."

Unperturbed he produced a pack of red-backed playing cards.

"Forgive me," and he inclined his head, "I anticipate myself. What I should have said was, you will become a great gin-rummy player. In this organization we are all experts. Much time is spent like this, travelling, waiting. You will find yourself becoming extremely skilful in a very short time. Shall we cut for deal?"

Laura shrugged, and cut the seven of hearts. Nagumi drew the four of spades, and handed her the pack with a small formal bow.

"Since there is only one chair," he said, sitting on the narrow bunk.

She had never been a particularly good dealer, and with the calm face watching she was even more clumsy than usual. Gradually she settled down to concentrate on the game. Nagumi won

97

easily, and she was glad to observe he did not bother to treat her lightly. There was no attempt to let her win, and if that was her object, she would have to do it herself.

They played another game, and another, Laura becoming deeply immersed, and making fewer mistakes. The sudden buzzing sound in the room came as an annoying interruption.

Nagumi sighed and put down his hand.

"I regret we shall not have time for more now. We must prepare to leave."

"I suppose there's no chance of seeing inside the cabin?" she asked tentatively. "I'd certainly love to get a look at those controls."

"Alas, I must regret. After this cruise, if all goes well, things will be easier. You will then be well on the way towards being one of us. Even then, there will be things not permitted. Even I, after all these years, do not have complete freedom. I trust you will understand our difficulties?"

"Oh yes, I understand."

Understand their difficulties? What harm could there be in looking at their silly controls? She'd seen plenty before. And in any case, what of her difficulties? Nobody seemed to pay very much attention to those. Outside he looked at her hair and said:

"Forgive me, but I think you might wish to attend to your hair. In here."

He opened another door, and she went in, chuckling to herself. She was getting to like the bland, polite Nagumi, who never seemed to be at a loss.

The Japanese was waiting outside for her when she emerged. They went back the way they had come, down the steel ladder to the floor of the ship, where the little Rondo waited like an old friend. The man was there again, the one who had secured the helicopter on their arrival. This time she did not speak, and the man appeared to nod with approval. Laura made to climb up into her passenger seat, but Nagumi said:

"No, not this time, Mrs. Kilburn. You will take the controls please."

Pleased, she ran around to the other

side, and climbed into the pilot's seat.

"I hope I can manage this all right," she told him, when he was beside her.

"I have no doubt of it, otherwise you would not be here," he replied gravely. "It will be good practice for you, and it will be good for our friends below. They will see I do not bring them an amateur. Please switch on."

She did so, and in the enclosed space the roar was two or three times as loud as it would normally be. Nagumi leaned close to her ear.

"In sixty seconds, the green and red lights will come on," he shouted. "When that happens, lift us no higher than three feet and wait."

She nodded, eyes glued to the small vital bulbs above her head. The seconds ticked away, her excitement mounting as her hands gripped the controls.

"Steady."

Nagumi put a reassuring hand on her shoulder. She tried to relax her tenseness. Then both lights appeared. Nagumi made lifting movements with his other hand.

The little Rondo rose smoothly from

the rubberized floor. That would be about three feet, she judged.

"Excellent," the familiar voice called in her ear. "Steady at that."

She nodded quickly, ridiculously pleased with herself for having performed such a simple feat. Nagumi pointed down, and she stared in horrified fascination as the floor of the flying boat appeared to fall away beneath them.

"Go down slowly, very slowly."

She did as he bid, worrying what would happen when they hit the air. After all, the flying boat was moving forward at probably two or three hundred miles an hour. Her forward speed was nil at the moment. The logical thing to happen would be that the tail half of the ship would slice them neatly in two when they were half-way out.

"Steady," encouraged Nagumi. "That is very good. See the light."

The green light was now flashing on and off, while the red continued to burn steadily.

"Excellent. Down three more feet."

She looked at him quickly, but the

impassive face looked back steadily. Then he nodded assurance, and pointed down. Reluctantly she did as he asked, waiting for the inevitable impact from behind. Nothing happened. Shaking her head in bewilderment, she looked around her. There was no doubt about it, they were riding along hanging half out of the flying boat. It was a technical impossibility.

"Down three more feet, and you will understand."

The normal pitch of Nagumi's voice made her aware sharply of how the engine noise had abated. Well, he'd been right so far. She lowered the Rondo even further from the mother ship, so that now only the vanes remained inside. And then she saw it. Projecting down from the giant fuselage was a metal screen protecting them from the oncoming airflow, and at the same time creating a vacuum which pulled them along. She turned to her passenger, grinning.

"Brilliant. It's positively brilliant."

"Now is the only tricky moment. You have sixty seconds to prepare yourself. Then the green light will go out, quite suddenly. You must at once give full throttle, and dive. Your door is locked securely?"

She checked quickly, knowing it to be unnecessary. Full throttle and then dive. Right. The green light disappeared. Laura slammed the throttle through the gate and dipped the helicopter's nose sharply. Then they were caught by the airflow and flung violently sideways. Laura wrestled furiously with the controls, using every skill she had to bring the little ship back on an even keel. Finally they were steady. She looked shamefacedly at Nagumi, who had lost none of his calm.

"Excellent, Mrs. Kilburn," he purred. "Really excellent. On my first attempt it took me far longer to correct. I lost almost five hundred feet. Very good indeed."

If that was a good one, she thought flippantly, I don't need to experience a bad one. Still, it was decent of Nagumi to be so generous about it.

"Where to now?" she asked.

He stared at the instrument panel then up at the night sky.

"Turn four degrees east, and fly level for two minutes. I fear we may have gone a little off course."

She followed the directions carefully.

"Now come down to seven hundred feet," he ordered. "Unless I am mistaken our friends will not be far away."

In the excitement Laura had forgotten the flying boat, and now stared upwards.

"No," chuckled Nagumi. "They have gone. Our new friends will be somewhere down there."

They flew along for another two minutes, with no result.

"Very well, we go round and try again."

One minute later the red bulb began to glow faintly.

"There they are. Fly on that signal. The moment it gets weaker, you are off course."

Laura concentrated on the glow. If it grew faint she turned the machine until brightness was restored. The light suddenly flickered, and remained on.

"We are here."

Nagumi pointed down, and they could

see three bright lights below, staggered into a flat triangle. Now she felt unsure of herself again. That was a ship, a small narrow structure in the Mediterranean. How could she possibly get them down on to it safely? It was all very well for this man to remain so calm. He didn't know what was going on in her stomach.

"Very well, Mrs. Kilburn, we will go down now."

And down they went, Laura blessing continually the ease with which the little helicopter responded to the controls. In no time they were within thirty feet of the deck, and then the green light flashed into life, burning with the steady brightness she already knew to indicate that everything was under control.

"After sixty seconds you will see the landing arrangements. Please go down immediately when you do."

She hoped he was right. All she could see at the moment was a well-cluttered deck with not much room anywhere to park a mini, let alone the Rondo. The seconds went slowly, then below her, the deck began to move. Not the ship, only the deck. It seemed to cant to one side somehow. Then it moved in the opposite direction, and she realized that in fact two huge sections were parting in the middle, and opening a yawning hole beneath.

"Quickly now."

She went down into the now brilliantly lit rectangle below. Soon the legs were resting once more on the same kind of rubber surface as had been on the flying boat. Looking to Nagumi for confirmation, Laura switched off. The green and red lights died, and above them the giant hatchways closed.

Nagumi nodded, pleased.

"I told you you could do it. Come, we have things to do."

They climbed out, and once again someone had materialized to make the helicopter fast.

"You don't want to advertise this machine, do you? Seems a shame."

Nagumi did not understand.

"I do not follow."

"Back at the house, you hide it on the roof. On the flying boat, you hide it in the fuselage, and now you hide it in the hold. Does no one ever see it?"

The Japanese permitted himself a small smile.

"It is no part of our intention that they do," he assured her. "Except for those we choose."

They went through a steel bulkhead, and into a lighted corridor.

"Are you ready to meet some people?"

People. She had begun to think her world was to be peopled only by the polite Nagumi.

"Lead the way," she replied.

He opened a door into a large room. There were several men, who stood at once when they saw her.

"Gentlemen, may I present, Mrs. Kilburn."

6

A man came towards her, both hands outstretched.

"Such a pleasure, my dear lady, a pleasure. John spoke to me of you often."

He was of medium height, sixtyish, with an aggresive black beard showing no signs of grey. His face beamed with welcome. She felt his genuine pleasure at meeting her, and was able to take his hands quite unselfconsciously.

"They call me Faust," he announced. "It is not my name of course, but these barbarians have little regard for names."

The other men grinned, grouping round them.

"Faust," said one, "you have no business to monopolize such a beautiful woman. Release her."

Faust did so at once, indicating the speaker.

"This is Emilio. He thinks he has a special talent with the ladies."

Laura could see that he might. He was tall and dark haired, with the brown skin and flashing smile of the true Mediterranean.

"And this is Gustav, and this one is Doc."

Gustav was a small solemn man in his thirties, who shook hands ceremoniously and gave Laura a half-bow. Doc, a grizzled wiry man of about fifty, stared into her eyes as they were introduced.

"Always look at the eyes," he informed her briefly in a soft Southern drawl. "You're a pretty healthy young lady."

"I hope so."

"Well now, this is nice. Come and sit down, my dear. We have one or two things to discuss."

Faust propelled her across to a chair, fussing over her.

"He fears for your balance," Emilio advised her gravely. "He is afraid this old tub might capsize."

"Capsize?" spluttered the bearded man. "Why, you never set foot on a more seaworthy ship. I should like to inform you — "

And he went off into a long tirade about the virtues of the ship. He was clearly either the owner, or the captain, Laura decided.

"He is normally very quiet," Nagumi whispered. "The sure way to annoy him is to criticize his ship."

The abuse seemed to have ended now. Faust gave one final glower towards Emilio, who seemed in no way perturbed.

"Nagumi, you have our instructions?"

"Yes."

Nagumi placed himself beside one wall, holding out a hand. Doc passed him a rolled paper which he pressed flat against the wall. It was an aerial photograph, and Laura recognized at once the village of Trois Bains, with the two hills clearly marked. The Japanese picked up a pencil from the table.

"In one hour, we shall be approximately here," and he jabbed at the sea at the bottom of the picture. Emilio, you will take the launch and four men. You will tie up here, half a mile east of the village. From there you will walk the rest. Avoid any contact with the

110

inhabitants. Not that there should be any around at four in the morning. You will take up positions around the jail, but do not approach. Your task, your sole task will be to prevent any of our friends from interfering with the operation. After it is complete, it will be for you to get the men back to the launch, again avoiding any contact, and return at once to the ship. It is clear?"

"Let me hear the rest first."

Emilio was not jovial now, but intent on the photograph, and what Nagumi was saying.

"We will give you twenty minutes start, then Mrs. Kilburn and I will come in the helicopter. If all goes well, you will reach the jail five minutes before us. I shall come down on the rope at the rear of the building close by the cell window, here. I shall only be able to deal with the escape of our friend. If your party Emilio, gets into any difficulty, I shall not help you. Also, I shall not permit our friend to join in either. If you get into trouble, it can only mean a few bruises, at the worst imprisonment. For our friend it is a question of making the acquaintance of Madame."

This brought a nodded frown from all the others. Of course, Laura recognized, Madame La Guillotine. The closeness of it all came home to her, as she looked at the intent faces around her.

"Of course. It is understood," agreed Emilio. "Just one point. The timing when we barricade the front door of the jail. If we do it too soon, they might either break out, or at least have time to make enough holes to get their carbines through. If this happens, some of us may come back a little heavier than we went."

"True. My recommendation is that you leave this until the last possible moment. There is nothing sinister about an approaching helicopter. It is only when we are almost overhead the gendarmes may think it worth coming out merely to take a look at us. If any of them does this, you will have to ensure they do not affect the enterprise."

Emilio smiled widely, and rolled his eyes. Nagumi went on.

"Now, the final stages. If anything goes wrong with the helicopter, it will be for you, Emilio, to get our friend back to the ship with you. Mrs. Kilburn and I will be otherwise engaged."

Laura looked at him anxiously. What did he mean? If something went wrong with the Rondo, then it was sensible that the prisoner should be taken back to the ship via the launch. But why shouldn't they go too, she and Nagumi? On what would they be 'otherwise engaged'?

The Japanese saw the expression on her face.

"You must understand Mrs. Kilburn, that this whole exercise has been mounted for one purpose only. What becomes of the rest of us is not greatly important. If we should fail, you and I, in our part, then we must do all in our power to see that Emilio does not."

"I quite see that," she replied doubtfully. "But what can we do that contributes? I mean once the chopper is out of action — "

"Quite," he interrupted, "But we shall not be. At least, I sincerely hope not. No, it will be for us to lead the chase. The police must think the prisoner is with us. If we are successful, then Emilio will have a very much better chance of getting him to the launch."

"I see."

The other men began to speak now, querying points of detail, but Laura had enough to think about already. Not that there was any need for alarm surely? What could possibly go wrong with the helicopter? It was in splendid trim, and the journey was a matter of a few miles only. No, she assured herself. It was quite right and proper that Nagumi should plan these alternatives, but the prospect of them ever being put into operation was decidedly remote. Nothing to worry about.

" — Mrs. Kilburn?"

Someone was speaking her name, and she came to with a jerk.

"Sorry," she stammered. "What was that?"

"I was saying," repeated Doc, "Have you had plenty of rest? Because if you are at all fatigued I can fix you up with a pill to see you through the next couple of hours."

"No, thank you. I had some rest this — yesterday afternoon."

"Then that is about it, thank you," said the one they called Faust. "I cannot ask you to drink to success, but I certainly can arrange for coffee and sandwiches."

Some of the others murmured approval. Laura, sensing that this was the time to relax, walked over and sat on a low leather chair. To her surprise, Doc came and perched himself on the arm.

"Smoke?"

She took one of the thick virginia cigarettes and he lit it from a leather-covered lighter.

"Your first cruise, Mrs. Kilburn," he said matter-of-factly. "How do you feel?"

"I don't really know," she admitted. "Until a few minutes ago, the whole business had a distinct flavour of the Arabian Nights. Now that it's actually about to start, I must say I'm a little jumpy."

"Good," he approved. "That is exactly the way you ought to be. I've seen a

115

lot of people go into action, both with this outfit, and shall we say more formal organizations? I like a man, excuse me, or a lady naturally, to be very slightly on edge. I've seen people who just shrugged off the whole thing as if they were going to somebody's tea party. Take it from me, it's a bad sign, particularly your first time out. These cool characters, the nerves of steel brigade, they're the first ones to blow up when it gets a little tough. You're doing fine."

He patted her on the shoulder, and she looked up at him. There was a look of kindness on the wise and weather-beaten face.

"Thank you," she acknowledged. "That did me more good than any of your pills. Tell me, did you know John, too?"

They were interrupted at that moment by Gustav, who had carried over coffee and a plate of sandwiches for Laura.

"I did not bring sugar," he informed her seriously, "Unless I make the mistake, the lady will not require it."

She realized that in their own way, these men were making a fuss of her.

Some day, she determined, she must ask Gustav exactly how he arrived at that conclusion.

"You're right," she nodded. "And thank you."

"You were asking about John," Doc said in a low voice. "Yes, I knew him. Knew him well. Matter of fact, we were together on one cruise, an emergency I recall, that blew up a few years ago. It was just three days before one of his finals. We spent all the time we weren't actually busy, grinding the stuff into his head. He'd brought his books with him."

"What sort of man was he?"

The question was out before Laura had realized it. Doc looked down at her oddly.

"Sounds a strange question, young lady, or may I call you Laura?"

"Please."

"A strange question. I was only his friend. You were his wife."

"True. Until yesterday I would have sworn no one knew John like I did. But now, in the face of all this, I begin to wonder whether I knew anything about him at all."

Doc didn't answer immediately, but appeared to be considering what Laura had said.

"Yes," he agreed at last, "I think I could understand how you might feel that way. But you oughtn't. The John you knew, the man you wanted to marry, that was the real John."

"And this?" She waved an arm.

"This was part of him too. But this was occasional, in his case. You were all the time. He felt like all of us here. We have votes, we can join societies, address meetings. We have all the apparent facilities of the modern world for expressing our point of view. But we can't do anything, not anything positive. There are lots of people like us in the world. Sometimes they do missionary work, sometimes they join what they feel to be the right army in some foreign war."

Laura looked up at him.

"You sound critical of such people," she chided. "Don't you think that in their own way they are doing something positive?"

"I do," he returned emphatically. "Most certainly I do. But what is the size of their effort? They are only men and women, as we all are. They can make life easier perhaps for one native village, after a lifetime's work. Or, if they're soldiers they can carry one gun, in a war involving possibly millions of guns. And they can die, of course. Many do, mostly unnecessarily, pointlessly."

Laura had always admired such people for their purpose, even if their convictions didn't always meet with her approval. To her it seemed that Doc belittled their efforts too easily.

"It's not difficult to dismiss what other people do," she said shortly.

"Take it easy," he advised mildly, "or you'll spill that coffee. How old are you Laura, twenty-two, twenty-three?"

"I'm twenty-five," she corrected, "And don't change the — "

"Twenty-five," he mused. "Wonderful. I don't suppose it'll be any surprise to you to know that I'm American?"

"Hardly. Georgia, I would guess."

"You would guess very well. When I was eighteen, I was in Spain fighting Franco. You could say that wasn't any of my business. At twenty I was in your R.A.F. Ever hear of the American Eagle Squadron?"

"Yes, naturally."

Laura was already wishing uncomfortably that she hadn't spoken so quickly.

"Well I guess you could also say your war was none of my business either — I had two wars, one after the other. Nearly eight years in all. And one thing I learned, slowly. I'd been on a losing side, and a winning side, so I was able to look at things both ways. The individual contribution is nothing against the whole backdrop. Oh, hallo Nagumi. Mrs. Kilburn and I were just getting acquainted."

The Japanese stood before them, looking at Laura.

"I am glad you are taking some refreshment, Mrs. Kilburn. But I'm afraid I must tear you away."

Laura got up, regarding the doctor levelly.

"Very well. Doc has just been prescribing for my judgement. I'm sure I shall find it valuable."

The lined face broke into a smile.

"Good luck, young woman. We must talk again."

Nagumi led her out of the cabin.

"You seem upset," he remarked. "And that is unusual. Doc is very much the person to put newcomers at their ease."

"It wasn't his fault," she admitted. "I just wish I hadn't been so quick with my opinions. Where to, now?"

"In here."

They were in a small cabin. He indicated a chair, and she sat down. Nothing was said, and she was beginning to wonder what was to happen, when the door opened and Faust joined them.

"Ah, there you are," he greeted. "One or two formalities, Mrs. Kilburn. First, your passports."

He handed them each a familiar booklet. Laura took hers slowly, and learned that she was Barbara Channing,

Irish, aged twenty-two. The photograph was good for a change. There was an entry visa for Spain inside the passport.

"Looks authentic enough," she remarked.

Faust seemed surprised.

"Well, I would hope so," he said. "Believe me, your own embassy could find nothing wrong with it. Please put it away."

Automatically, she began to unbutton the left breast pocket of her suit.

"No," corrected Nagumi. "The other pocket, please."

That was the second time he'd done that, she recalled. If he went on like this she'd be all bulgy on one side. People would think she was deformed or something.

Faust now produced two cardboard boxes, and slid one across to each of them.

"Inside you will find a garment. It is to be worn next to the skin, please. Although not one hundred per cent, it is the most advanced bullet-proof material yet produced. It will stop almost anything except a ninety degree hit from a machine gun. This is some of our most valuable equipment. You will please treat it with great care, and return it to me immediately the cruise is completed."

Laura noted thankfully that Nagumi made no attempt to unfasten his box. This comrades in arms stuff was all very well up to a point, but she didn't feel she was yet so comradely that she could face changing her clothes in front of these strangers. Faust had been watching her.

"You will be able to change in a few minutes Mrs. Kilburn. In addition, you will both please place these extra thicknesses over your hearts."

He pushed two thick wads of the material towards them. Nagumi lifted his and tucked it carefully into his left breast pocket, smiling faintly at Laura as he did so. The stuff didn't look anything special, she thought. Rather like an overlarge handkerchief of some material which could almost be oiled silk. It fitted neatly into the empty pocket, and now she felt balanced. In fact, she thought smugly, she must look quite interesting.

"And now," Faust looked at the Japanese, "if you will forgive me, I would like a private word with our new recruit. She will join you at the helicopter in fifteen minutes."

After the door closed behind Nagumi, Faust said quietly:

"This is part of our normal routine, young lady. At the moment, you are almost one of us, not quite. In an hour or two, you will be committed. If there is any feeling on your part, that you regret having come this far, it is not too late for you to step aside. You will be returned to your home, and that will end the matter."

"But the operation," she protested. "Surely I'm needed?"

"Needed yes, but you are not the pivot on which the whole cruise rotates. It would be inconvenient, extremely so, if you should decide not to go ahead, but the cruise will still take place as planned. What is your answer?"

The silence was oppressive in the small cabin. Laura thought hard before replying. Till now there had been so much excitement, so much to learn and do, that she hadn't had much time for thinking. And, she admitted privately, she had shied away from much more than a passing thought or two anyway. Had Faust not put it to her baldly, the way he now did, she would have allowed herself to be swept along quite happily throughout the actual cruise. But now she was being compelled to examine the situation coldly. And she sat quite still, knowing that this was not a case of argument and counter-argument with some logic on both sides. It was a simple matter of emotion versus reason. There was not one sound reason why she should have anything to do with this business at all. In fact, everything reasonable shouted against it. On the other hand, here was her chance to help the man who had avenged John. And when you have said that, she admitted, you have said everything.

"I'll go, of course," she announced.

Faust nodded, as though that was the answer he had expected.

"I am pleased you did not reply at once," he said gravely. "It is a very serious decision and it requires serious consideration. Very well. I will wait outside to give you a chance to put on this — um — garment, and then I will take you to join Nagumi."

He went out, and Laura opened the cardboard container. There was a kind of shortie shift inside, with nothing of Bond Street or Paris about it. Quickly she unzipped her boiler suit, and slipped the thing over her head. It was cold on her skin, but not an unpleasant feeling, and within seconds she was ready to leave. Faust nodded, and took her by the arm.

"A final word," he muttered, as they walked along. "If anything should go wrong with our arrangements, and the gendarmes get free, they may well use their firearms. They may even, and I hate the thought, shoot the escaping prisoner. But whatever happens, you will not return their fire. They are honest men, carrying out their proper duty, and we have no

126

quarrel with such. It is understood?"

"Quite."

Nagumi was standing beside the helicopter, talking to a man Laura hadn't seen before.

"The timing?" queried Faust.

"Emilio's party left twenty three-minutes ago," Nagumi replied.

"Splendid. Well, I mustn't detain you. Good luck."

And with that, he walked away. It was all very casual, thought Laura. She and Nagumi might be off to hunt for a new hat for Easter. She didn't know quite what she'd expected, but certainly something more dramatic, something less prosaic than Faust's "I mustn't detain you". Climbing into the pilot's seat she took a quick look round.

"O.K.?" queried the Japanese beside her.

"O.K."

She started the engine, and the little machine began to throb. Nagumi waved his hand, and above their heads, the roof split neatly and stars appeared in a thin line, widening as they watched. All the lights went off now and above the control panel the familiar green and red of the Z-box glowed. Nagumi put a hand on her arm and squeezed gently.

"Good luck, Mrs. Kilburn. Let's go."

7

The ship dwindled away beneath them, and Laura saw the shoreline over to her left. Down there, the fishermen of Trois Bains would be snoring peacefully, and so with any luck would the gendarmes, or most of them. Emilio and the others would be in position if there had been no snags, and all she had to do was drop in and empty the jail. She came down to five hundred feet as she crossed the coastline and even with the few lights burning at that hour, there was no mistaking the layout of the village. There was very little cloud, and she peered through the perspex for her first sight of the hill.

"Throttle back, please."

Nagumi's voice interrupted her thoughts. Now he pulled back the door beside him and scanned the earth below. Round his waist, the silken cord was securely fixed, and even if he fell out he would come to no harm. All that would happen would

129

be a free fall of about six feet before the line pulled up taut, and he would merely dangle helplessly below the machine until Laura either brought him back up or lowered him. She eyed the small but powerful winch which she would have to operate soon.

"There."

Nagumi pointed, and Laura was just in time to see a quick red glow, which as quickly disappeared.

"That's Emilio. And there's the hill."

She could see it now, squat and brooding in the faint light from the stars. The jailhouse would be halfway up the shelving side. As the thought entered her mind, a faint yellow glow appeared. That would be a window.

"Come down to twenty feet, and start paying me out."

As she lowered the helicopter, Laura could make out faint shadows on the side of the hill, near the jail. Emilio's men, making sure the guards stayed inside.

"Right."

The Japanese stepped carefully out into

the sky, lowering himself until the slack on the line was almost payed out, then dropped the other couple of feet. The helicopter swayed slightly, and Laura hung on. They were directly behind the jail now, and Nagumi waved his hand to indicate he was ready. She switched on the winch, at bottom speed, and slowly the dangling man descended to the ground. The helicopter was rock-steady as his feet lightly touched the earth. At once he freed himself, and ran towards the jail, pulling the rope with him. A hand came through the barred window and grabbed the rope. The man inside wound it quickly around each bar in turn. There was no sign of any activity elsewhere, as Laura peered anxiously around. Nagumi was waving now. Time to remove the window. Laura crossed her fingers, and slipped the winch control to 'Rewind'. The helicopter juddered, stayed firm. Then, very slowly, the tough silk began to inch its way on to the spindle. There was a splintering crash below, and the waiting Japanese had to fling himself sideways, as the barred window came away en bloc. At once Laura switched off. Another man appeared now, at the gaping hole in the wall, pulling himself awkwardly through and landing unsteadily. Nagumi had the rope free, and quickly wound it round the prisoner. Together they ran directly beneath the helicopter and Nagumi signalled. Again the winch moved into rewind, but too slowly. The prisoner shouted something Laura could not hear above the noise of the engine, but she guessed the import and accelerated the winch. Seconds later a head appeared above the bottom of the door, and a man scrambled inside.

"Hi," he snapped.

At once, he set about untying himself, and tossing the rope back down to Nagumi.

"Well come on dammit," he barked shortly. "Let the winch down."

Laura flushed in the darkness, but did at once as he bid. He was quite right, of course. No point in rescuing him, only to leave the Japanese behind in his place. Still, a quick thank you would not have been out of place.

"He's got it. Steady now. O.K. Haul him up."

Again she followed automatically. Then there was a new sound. Even above the engine there was no mistaking the sharp crack of rifles.

"Speed it up for God's sake. The guy's a sitting duck."

She accelerated, and Nagumi quickly appeared, to be hauled unceremoniously inboard by the stranger. Once his legs were in, the ex-prisoner gave a great whoop, turned and clapped Laura hard on the back.

"O.K. Pop. Let's go home."

She swung the machine round and climbed steeply away. Her shoulder, she was quite convinced, was broken. And certainly she'd never been called Pop before. Nagumi was seated now, with the newcomer on the flat box behind him.

"Well, well, you old lotus eater. Never thought I'd be glad to see your ugly mug again. Who's the new buddy?"

The man behind accompanied this with another thump on the back, but this time it was Nagumi's turn to suffer. He didn't

133

seem to mind though, and his voice was full of pleasure as he replied:

"Mike, I swear, one of these days you are going to get yourself in a spot."

"A spot?" was the indignant reply. "A spot he says. Those guys were only going to cut off my head, is all. How tough do things have to get to suit you?"

"Tough?" scoffed the Japanese. "It was a breeze. You knew we'd get you out. Yours was the easy part."

"Easy? Listen to this guy. I tell you my poor old head hadn't felt easy in a week. Does this guy talk?"

Laura smiled grimly to herself. The noisy Mike would be quite abashed when he found out he was talking about a woman. To her surprise Nagumi did not enlighten him.

"Oh yes, he talks," he confirmed. "We call him K at the moment. First cruise, you understand."

"Oh."

That seemed to satisfy Mike, who patted Laura more gently on the shoulder.

"It's O.K. pal. I remember what it's

134

like. You did fine, and I want to thank you."

Laura nodded. She was at six hundred feet now, and clear of the coast.

"Say, anybody got a smoke? I mean, those French cigarettes are all very dandy, but I sure could use some cool Virginia."

Laura dug around in her pocket, produced a pack, and handed it over her shoulder.

"Thanks. Well, what's the pitch?"

"We have a ship a little way off the coast."

"Fine. Say this is a good smoke. I could use some decent food too. Not that those guys didn't feed me, but it wasn't exactly the Ritz. Nagumi, you know what's in mind for me?"

"Not yet. There will have to be a conference of course."

Laura concentrating on her controls, only half listened to what was being said. Anxiously she checked the compass again.

"We should be over the ship," she announced. "There's no sign of it."

"A dame," ejaculated Mike.

"Never mind that, look for the ship," counselled the Japanese. "Sweep around Mrs. Kilburn, she may have drifted."

She brought the little machine lower as she covered the area in a narrow circle. Even if they couldn't see the ship, the Z-box should have been shining its green light, at least for the past two minutes. Trying to sound matter of fact, she said:

"I have about fuel enough for one and a half hours' flying time. Do we continue to search?"

Nagumi's reaction was instant.

"No. There must have been trouble. Fly south south east while I work out a proper bearing."

She did as he said automatically, wondering where they would eventually come down.

"What about the team on the ground?" queried Mike. "Shouldn't we go back and make sure they're not in any trouble?"

"No," again the decision was immediate. "Emilio is in charge. He has been in difficulties before. He has radio contact with the ship and they are better able to help than we. Our job was to get you away. We will finish it. Mrs. Kilburn, here is our bearing."

"We're heading for Hugo's place, I imagine," asked Mike. "Kind of risky isn't it?"

"It cannot be avoided. In any case I think it less risky than landing in the desert and trying to walk home. Keep your mixture as thin as possible, Mrs. Kilburn, and we shall just make it."

Laura adjusted the mixture control, devoting her complete faculties to flying the machine, and determined not to think about what would be the alternative if they didn't just make it. There was no more talking now, each busy with private thoughts. Then there were lights, well over to the left, and at least ten miles away. Laura tried to recall her skimpy knowledge of the Mediterranean.

"Those lights," she pointed. "Would that be Majorca?"

"No, Mrs. Kilburn," corrected the Japanese. "Providing we are on course, and I see we are, that is Minorca. Majorca is dead ahead and we shall be skirting the island in the next few minutes."

She thought quickly.

"But surely, if we do that, there's no more land until the north coast of Africa? I haven't enough fuel to — "

"No, you are not quite correct. There are a number of small islands in the Balearic group, some too small to justify inclusion in ordinary maps. Due south of Majorca and eight or ten miles from it lies the island of Cabrera. That is where we are heading."

"Hasn't the lady been told any of this?" demanded Mike suddenly.

He'd been silent for so long, Laura had imagined he'd fallen asleep.

"It was not considered to be necessary," contributed Nagumi. "Particularly on a first cruise."

"Wonder what happened to frighten the ship off that way."

The lights of Majorca were coming into view now, away to the right. Laura had spent a holiday there once with John, and felt a momentary sadness looking down at the sleeping island. There was a hand on her shoulder. Nagumi said:

"Please do not be offended, but I think I ought to take over now. Our place on Cabrera is very small, and there will be no lights."

She climbed out of the seat at once to let him move in. Then she stepped over beside Mike, squatting on the floor. It was too dark to see his face clearly.

"Mrs. Kilburn, that's what Nagumi called you?"

"Yes. I'm Laura Kilburn."

"Knew a man named Kilburn once. Doctor, name of John. Any kin of yours?"

"I'm his — " then she paused correcting herself, "I was his wife."

"Well, well," he muttered. "Imagine."

Impulsively she reached out and took his hand, clasping it warmly. "I know what you did," she told him. "For me to try thanking you would be so inadequate. But I want you to know how I feel."

He squeezed her hand in return.

"That was a lousy break about John. He talked about you a lot. By the way, I'm Mike Monahan, thirty, and I smoke too much."

"We are getting close to the island. Mrs. Kilburn, be good enough to let Mike have your gun."

She did as Nagumi asked, handing the weapon gingerly across.

"Guns?" she queried. "Surely they can't be needed?"

"Well now Laura," said Mike slowly. "Seeing what lovely people we all are, you'll find this hard to believe. But the sad fact is, there are people who don't like us. Quite a lot of people, and they have guns."

The fuel gauge was hovering around zero, and Laura was wondering whether the helicopter would make their destination.

"We're here. I'll come down to fifty feet."

They all strained their eyes into the blackness below.

"Man, I couldn't see if they had a squadron of tanks down there."

Nagumi lowered the machine gradually, until they were no more than a dozen feet from the ground. Laura could now see that a small square had been cut into the side of a hill. A building, not much

140

more than a hut, stood to one side.

"O.K. I can't see anything. Let's go down."

The helicopter landed softly in the square. Laura made to get out, but felt a restraining hand on her arm.

"Ladies last," remonstrated Mike.

He and Nagumi jumped clear together, landing on all fours and remaining motionless. Nothing happened. Gradually, they straightened up and began walking towards the hut. Laura climbed out now, following along behind them. At the doorway, Mike motioned Laura to one side, while Nagumi knocked loudly.

"Esteban," he called.

After he spoke the second time, the door opened.

"Senior Nagumi," said a delighted voice.

Out from the hut shambled a fat hulk of a man who proceeded to throw his arms around the Japanese with evident affection. The two laughed and pummelled at each other, chattering away in Spanish. Then Esteban saw Laura and Mike, and shook hands effusively. Bowing deeply to Laura, he said something to Nagumi which brought a quick chuckle in response.

"What did he say?" Laura wanted to know.

"He said I have no right to bring such a beautiful lady to his house without warning him."

Laura's knowledge of Spanish was confined to odd words she had picked up from movies about Mexico.

"Gracias señor," she said smiling.

Esteban pumped her hand even harder. Then Nagumi placed an arm on his shoulder and led him away, speaking quickly and seriously.

"Mr. Nagumi seems to have an old friend," she said to Mike.

"That is putting it mild, lady. The old boy has a son, Miguel. There was a little excitement here once, couple of years ago, and Nagumi saved the lad's life. Esteban would cut off his arm if Nagumi told him to."

The two men finished their talk and came back.

"Everything is in order," reported

Nagumi. "Esteban has had no visitors, and our stores have not been touched. He wanted us to have some food, but I've explained we have to be moving on. Mainly for your sake, Mrs. Kilburn. Esteban is a splendid fellow, but undoubtedly the worst cook in the world."

The old Spaniard disappeared into the hut, and came out again with a big lantern, leading them into the thick bushes beside the hut. After twenty yards or so, he stopped, handing the lantern for Laura to hold. Pulling aside a large tarpaulin, he indicated a pile of tins and boxes.

"All the comforts of home," explained Mike. "We keep emergency fuel here, and enough food to feed a dozen people for a week."

The men each picked up two of the fuel cans, and the little party made its way back to the helicopter. Laura held the lantern high while the men tipped the fuel into the machine. In this way they made three trips, and then the job was done.

"Time to be moving on," announced Nagumi.

The first pale streaks of dawn had already put in an appearance by the time they were ready to leave. There was a good deal more handshaking and back slapping from Esteban. They climbed aboard, Nagumi taking the controls, and after a final wave to the old man, they lifted off, heading due south.

"You ever been to Africa, lady?" asked Mike.

"No, but it looks as though that's about to be corrected," she replied.

"That it is."

8

They maintained a steady course, and soon it was full daylight. Below, the sea shimmered under the early sun, and Laura found it difficult to keep awake. Beside her, Mike smoked incessantly, but there was not much conversation. The sun picked up strength and it began to get very stuffy in the confined cabin. Laura wished she could take off some clothes. The black overalls had been ideal for the middle of the night, but they were not designed for the heat of an African day.

"Have we much further to go?" She ventured.

Nagumi shook his head.

"I would estimate about another thirty minutes," he replied.

"Always assuming we shall be welcome when we get there."

He didn't explain his last remark, but Laura was becoming accustomed to the way these people worked. Eagerly, she scanned the horizon for her first glimpse of the continent. And then her heart leaped as a thin line appeared in the distance.

"We're a sitting duck up here."

They were the first words Mike had spoken for hours, and Laura started at the sudden ejaculation.

"I don't understand you."

He made no reply, staring morosely out of the window. The coastline was much closer now, and Laura could see no sign of life, or even vegetation. Nothing but sand and rock in any direction.

"I think we had better go down and talk," said Nagumi.

He swung the little helicopter over the low cliffs and brought her gently down. A fine flurry of sand swirled around as the machine landed, sinking several inches up the landing wheels.

"Let us get out and stretch our legs."

Laura jumped down, and stared about her. Her first reaction was one of great peace. The land was so barren and silent, it made her feel that she wanted to remain forever, losing herself in its timelessness.

"Like it?"

Mike's voice at her shoulder.

"M'm," she nodded. "I don't remember being so profoundly affected by a place before. Think of the great armies that have passed here, Greeks, Romans, Egyptians, Moors. I could spend all day here, just thinking and imagining."

"We may have to, if I know what's in Nagumi's mind."

The Japanese joined them then.

"Mrs. Kilburn," he said seriously, "I find myself in a rather delicate position. It is the custom, indeed it is a rule, that people on their first cruise are permitted to see only what is essential for the successful completion of the mission. Already I have broken that rule by letting you see our supply point on Cabrera."

"I don't think you had much alternative, did you? It was either that or land in the Mediterranean. Or is automatic suicide a rule, too?"

He smiled non-committally.

"That is a point," he admitted. "Nevertheless, as I say, strictly speaking I have broken a rule."

"You wouldn't have had to if the ship hadn't gone off and left us. What I don't understand is how she got away so quickly. And for that matter, why she went at all."

Mike chuckled.

"Lady, if you ever saw the engines on that old tub, you wouldn't wonder at her speed. Why, she could outdistance — "

"Mike," snapped Nagumi.

"Oh, sorry, you're quite right. I guess being in the pen has softened my brain."

Laura lit a cigarette, and was surprised at how few were left in the packet. Mike shrugged guiltily.

"As to the reason for the ship's departure, that brings me to my next problem, Mrs. Kilburn. They would not have gone without excellent reasons. There are only two possibilities. One, they could have been found by a naval vessel, and had to depart. There is a good deal of naval activity in those waters because of the smuggling between North Africa and the Mediterranean ports."

"And the other possibility?"

"They could have been found by some of our friends."

Nagumi's face was very serious as he said this.

"By friends, I gather you really mean enemies?" Laura asked.

"Yes. They are, regrettably, well equipped. Almost as well as we ourselves. Sooner than face a confrontation, our people would have slipped away."

"You see honey, if they hung around, with us about due, the other guys would have seen us coming in. The helicopter is a beautiful piece of equipment, but a marksman could have brought us down with a sling shot almost."

That was Mike's contribution, and it only took one look at his face for Laura to realize he was not joking.

"I see," she commented gravely. "Well gentlemen, where do we go from here? There isn't all that much fuel left, unless you have another dump somewhere close by."

"That's precisely my problem," admitted Nagumi. "Perhaps you will excuse us if Mike and I talk in private."

The two men strolled away, conversing quietly. Laura watched them go, wondering what it was all about. Whatever it was, she hoped it wouldn't take long to decide. All she could concentrate on was the thought of getting into some cool clothes. If she could just get rid of the skin bullet-proof thing, that would be a wonderful start. Ah, they were coming back. Nagumi spoke first.

"Mrs. Kilburn, we have decided. We are going to take what I believe to be an unprecedented step. The normal drill after a first cruise, is for you to be judged by at least two members of the Council. It is they who decide whether you are acceptable for further service. We are neither of us members. And so we have to decide for ourselves. It is most irregular."

Neither of them seemed particularly happy about what they were doing, and Laura suspected they might have trouble over it later.

"Very well. And what have you decided?"

"Mrs. Kilburn," and she was taken

aback by the sudden formality of Mike's address, "you had better sit down for a moment."

Obediently, she sank down on to the warm sand. The men sat also, the three of them making a stiff-backed triangle.

"The fact is, Mrs. Kilburn, that recruits are usually taken on a first cruise because it is something in which the Council feel they have some personal involvement. They are normally also required to incriminate themselves, as you did last night. This makes it unlikely that they will wish to reveal the circumstances to anyone else."

"Oh."

Put like that, Laura did not like the description too well.

"If they do not wish to continue, or if not considered suitable, then they revert to their normal lives, and the whole affair is forgotten. Ordinarily, you would have returned to your flat today, and if you indicated that you were interested in further work for us, you would be advised of the decision in due course."

"But I can scarcely be expected to walk

151

home from somewhere in Morocco."

"Precisely. Therefore, we now have two alternatives. One is for you to remain here until Mike and I are able to have you picked up. The difficulty there is that I have no idea how long that might be. One day, two days, I cannot tell."

"That doesn't sound so bad until you consider what it means," interjected Mike. "You'd have no shelter, no food. That sun might look pretty, but it's a killer when there isn't any shade. Plus, this whole area has nomads roaming around, and it might not be too healthy if any of that bunch found you."

"You paint a fairly gloomy picture of the first alternative," nodded Laura. "May I please hear the second?"

The Japanese waited a few moments before replying.

"The second is for you to state now that you wish to join us permanently. Do not decide hastily. Once admitted, you will learn many things. Things of great importance and secrecy. Things which we cannot risk having revealed to the outside world. You will be expected to

152

undertake whatever mission is selected for you, and you will not hold back. These affairs are mainly hazardous, and frequently unpleasant. Apart from taking into account the fact that you are a woman, you will be treated no differently from the rest. And there can be no withdrawal from us, without the express permission of the Council."

"I see."

Laura was silent after that. She was not at all certain she relished the prospect painted by Nagumi. The rescue of Mike, who had avenged her husband's murder, was something she had wanted to do. In fact she had jumped at the chance. But to give up her comfortable life, her friends, her flat, and on top of that to risk her life as a matter of routine, that was a very different matter.

"How long may I have to think about it, please?"

"I am sorry, but not more than one half-hour," replied Nagumi.

"May I ask something?"

"Please."

"What is entailed for me in this? I

mean, is it like joining the army? Will I be leaving home for good, or what?"

It was Mike who answered this time.

"No, that isn't the way it works, usually. There are a lot of people of course, who are engaged the whole time. But you would be a kind of reserve operative. That is to say, you'd lead your own life, but you'd have to be ready to leave at say an hour's notice, for maybe a couple of months, anywhere in the world. Does that answer you?"

"Yes. But how could I possibly explain sudden absences?"

"All our people have unbreakable cover," explained Nagumi. "You will be furnished with an identity which would make such a way of life perfectly credible."

"Thank you. May I go away and think?"

She left the two men sitting there, and walked off into the desert. It was ridiculous of course. She was Laura Kilburn, a person of small but established reputation. She had a life to lead, a normal life with a job and other interests.

It was no part of her future to be risking her life, and carrying guns, and the rest of it. Then she thought deeper. What future? And come to that, what did she mean by her present normal life. There could be no real future with John dead. Oh there would be a man, some time later, perhaps more than one. She was a healthy vital female, and her own honesty told her she couldn't live on memory for ever. But so far as her future, Laura Kilburn's future was concerned, it would hold no real purpose or meaning, without John. As for her present so-called normal life, what was normal about being shut in every night, sleepless till the small hours, waiting for sheer exhaustion to overcome the aching emptiness? Not many people would consider that normal, she fancied. And so she paced and fretted, arguing with herself.

She used up the whole thirty minutes in this way, finally trudging back through the wearying sand, to where the two men now sat, taking advantage of the small shade provided by the helicopter.

Nagumi stood as she approached.

155

"Before you speak Mrs. Kilburn, let me tell you one further thing. As I explained, Mike and I are acting without authority. We hope the Council will understand that we had no choice. However, if it should turn out that we made a bad decision today, it will go very hard with us."

"I second that," agreed Mike. "And what's more, we shall be expected to deal with the matter personally."

"Deal with the matter?" echoed Laura vaguely. "What precisely does that mean?"

"It means, lady," returned Mike slowly, "that we would have to kill you. Please don't put us to that trouble."

It was as much the matter of factness of his delivery, as the actual words, which stopped Laura in her tracks. There was no evading the fact that these men were totally serious. But her gaze did not waver as she stared at each in turn.

"I understand. It makes no difference to my choice. I will join you."

They looked at each other, nodding. Then Nagumi held out his hand in a formal fashion.

"Welcome, Mrs. Kilburn. May you

have the lives of a cat."

She shook hands ceremoniously, then with Mike who repeated the same words.

Well, she thought, I seem to have done it this time.

9

"Sit down Mrs. Kilburn," invited Nagumi. "We will tell you the plan we have in mind."

That was a promising start, at least. Hitherto, she'd only been given such information as was absolutely essential to the next stage of the operation. Obviously, once in, you were in.

"A few miles along the coast there is one of the residences of Hugo Holloway. You are perhaps familiar with the name?"

"The millionaire? Or should I say multi-millionaire?"

"That is the man."

She was intrigued. Holloway was one of the flamboyant figures of the twentieth century. The stories of his colourful career were legion. How much was fact, and how much embroidery, Laura had no way of knowing. He was reputed to have been a boxer, deckhand, ex-army major, an official of the United Nations organization. Certainly he was now a producer of epic movies, of the kind that cost five million dollars and gross twenty-five, a good part of which found it's way back to Holloway. He was in his forties, and had the reputation of being a hell-raiser. Divorced twice, no three times, and constantly being photographed with starlets and models, and other euphemistically described partners. That was someone she'd look forward to meeting.

"Mr. Holloway is one of us," continued Nagumi. "He is in fact a member of the Council."

She looked up in surprise. Mike winked at her solemnly.

"You live and learn in this business," he informed her.

"What we fear, is that he might have had visitors. The fact of the disappearance of the ship is disturbing. If the opposition knew of the ship, it is just as conceivable they might have learned about Mr. Holloway. If they have, our visit might be short. And painful."

"What he means honey is, if the rover

boys have captured the castle, they ain't going to put out any red carpet when we show."

"Exactly," concurred Nagumi. "In fact, Mrs. Kilburn, it will be downright unhealthy."

She nodded, thinking.

"And there's no alternative?"

"None."

"Then gentlemen, had we not better proceed?"

Mike grinned broadly, and even the impassive Japanese allowed himself a fleeting smile.

"You will please take the controls. We have only two guns, and you will forgive my saying so, both Mike and I are better shots. It will be preferable for us to be free to deal with — um — anything that needs dealing with."

She pulled herself up into the ship, the metal rim of the door almost blistering her hands with the sun's heat. Inside the chopper the atmosphere was like a furnace. Perspiration rolled off her, and her fingers were so slippery she had difficulty in grasping the controls.

"That's why we had to get a move on," explained Mike. "Later in the day it gets hot around here."

They lifted off, Nagumi telling her to steer along the coastline.

"We should be there in less than an hour."

He had to put his face close to her ear to combat the roar of the engine. Laura nodded to show she'd heard. They opened everything that would open, grateful for the slightest breath of wind that found its way into the stuffy cabin. Below the cliffs to the right, the Mediterranean sparkled, lapping enticingly against the stony beaches. That's where I ought to be, thought Laura. It was as though Mike could read her mind.

"You a swimmer?" he shouted.

"A little."

She hadn't swum for a long time. When John was alive it had been different. Then she noticed that the cliffs were declining, no longer the imposing heights they'd started from. Soon they were flying over almost flat ground, parallel with the sea.

161

Nagumi put a hand on her shoulder, and she turned her head.

"Not long now," he told her. "I should go down almost to ground level."

She did as he said. Judging by the fuel indicator, they had better be close to their destination, if they didn't want to walk the last part of the journey. Then she saw something, up ahead, a break in the flat monotony, some kind of building with palm trees. Laura pointed impulsively, and the men nodded.

"Straight over the wall, Mrs. Kilburn. There is room to land in the courtyard. Reduce speed. We will go in very slowly, and be ready to come out very fast. Do not concern yourself with anything except flying the machine."

Nagumi waited to ensure she had understood, then squatted behind her on the floor by the open doorway. Laura noted with rising excitement that he was holding his gun, and a quick check told her that Mike was doing the same thing at the other door. They were almost up to the house now, a startling white building looking like something from a film scene,

162

rather than a place where anyone lived. The wall was high, about fifteen feet, Laura elevated the nose of the helicopter slightly to ensure clearance. Then they were over, and she was hovering above a paved courtyard, with a fountain at either end. There was room to land six helicopters if necessary. There was no sign of life. Nagumi pointed for her to go down. Gently, she lowered the little machine to the ground. As she made to switch off the engine, Mike's hand closed over her own.

"Not yet," he cautioned.

A white-robed figure in a red fez appeared by one of the fountains. In his arms was cradled a sub-machine gun. At once Mike leaped to the ground.

"Hey Kish — Kish, is that you?"

The Arab studied the newcomer, then broke into a run, lowering the weapon.

"Okay, honey. Switch off. We're home."

Laura cut the engine, watching the tall man running.

"Kish-Kish you old bastard. Put that thing down."

The face of the running man broke into

a wide white smile.

Then he and Mike were hugging each other, and banging one another on the back. Nagumi joined them, he and the Arab shaking hands delightedly. She thought it was safe to climb down now, and the robed man studied her seriously.

"Kish-Kish, this is Mrs. Kilburn," introduced Nagumi. "She is one of us."

"The lady is most welcome."

The Arab placed his hands together as if in prayer, and accorded Laura a short bow of the head. Somewhat non-plussed she said "How do you do?"

"C'mon, you desert heathen, take us to your leader," Mike enjoined.

Kish-Kish led the way across the courtyard. As they passed the fountain it took all Laura's will-power not to jump into it. A long shady verandah ran along the back of the house. They went up flat, wide steps into a low, cool room.

"Please, I will tell the master."

The Arab left them. Laura stared around wonderingly at the rich furnishings of the room.

"The only place I've ever seen anything like this was in the Palace of Versailles."

"Mr. Holloway is a man of great taste for fine things," agreed Nagumi. "It would have been a pity to have lost all this to our enemies."

That brought her back to the present.

"Yes, I wanted to ask about that. Supposing we had been on the wrong side? One man with a tommy gun doesn't seem to be much to defend this place."

The men laughed. Mike took her arm and turned her towards the window by which they had entered.

"Down there," he pointed. "Half way down the courtyard, there is a thick bush. See?"

"Yes, I see it."

"Also, another one similar on the opposite side. Those dear lady, are gun emplacements. In each there is a man, sitting behind twin Browning .303's. Between them they have enough fire-power to eliminate half a regiment."

She shuddered, and turned away.

"Do you think it will be possible to get a glass of water?" she queried.

"Not yet," demurred Nagumi. "On arrival after a cruise, unless one is wounded, it is a rule that we report first."

The silent Kish-Kish had reappeared.

"If you will please follow."

They walked behind him, through a maze of stone archways and passages, coming at last to huge double doors. The Arab knocked once, twice, then pushed the door wide. They all went into a large room, but Laura did not take it in at once. Her attention was focused on the man at the window. He was broad, powerful-looking figure, with thick black hair. She had seen enough newspaper pictures to know that this was Holloway.

"Nagumi, Mike," he boomed, holding out both hands. "And who is this young lady?"

"This is Mrs. Kilburn, Hugo," introduced Nagumi. "She helped us get Mike out."

"Yes, I know that." Holloway stared at her curiously. "But what's she doing here?"

"Well, we have to tell you about that," interjected Mike.

"That you do, lad, that you do. However let us remember she is a guest."

Holloway came up to her, holding out a great hand. She was relieved to find he did not crush her own. The newspapers did not do him justice, she decided.

"You must be hot and in need of refreshment," he said, his eyes boring into her. "Kish-Kish will take you to where you can freshen up. Oh, and if you'd like to get out of those clothes for a while, he can fix that too. I had a visitor not long ago, about your size. An Italian countess, whose beauty, I am happy to say, was exceeded only by her lack of discretion."

She flushed under the direct gaze, and followed Kish-Kish out of the room. He led her up a sweeping staircase, past several rooms before coming to a white painted door.

"In here please. I bring food."

She nodded gratefully, and went in. It was a large airy room, simply but

167

comfortably furnished. There was a built-in wardrobe occupying the whole length of one wall. Tiredness overcome immediately by female curiosity, Laura pulled one of the doors smoothly sideways, and all but gaped. There were enough clothes, freshly pressed and hung, to cover any three women for the rest of their lives. She pushed back hanger after hanger, inspecting, feeling and making very little progress. It was exactly like being in a big department store. Except that here, every dress was different, and the briefest look would tell anyone that none of this had ever originated from a multiple retailer.

She had already found at least six dresses which would suit her admirably when there was a quiet tapping at the door. It was Kish-Kish, carrying a silver tray, over which he bowed as he came in and set it down on a small table. Laura thanked him and he went away. The food looked good, salad sandwiches, a piece of gorgonzola, fruit and a half bottle of Algerian wine. Going to the door, she found a bolt which she pushed home.

Then, off came the black overall and the now-detested bullet-proof shirt. From the wardrobe she removed a green cotton housecoat and slipped it on, revelling in the sudden freedom of her body. Hungry as she was, she must have at least a wash first. There was another door leading from the bedroom, and opening this she got another surprise. It was a bathroom, but unlike any she'd ever seen outside magazine pages. A sunken oval of pink marble, with three steps leading down into it. The walls were all mirrors, and along the rim of the bath was an elaborate array of oils and perfumes. The bath was already half-filled with warm scented water and Laura did not hesitate to remove the coat and step down into the inviting depths.

Twenty minutes later she emerged reluctantly, all tiredness now replaced by a gentle sensuous languor. As she sat on the bed, nibbling at the sandwiches she found herself speculating about the Italian countess. And, to judge by that range of clothes, a number of other females who had preceded her into that bath. One thing was certain, she reminded herself sharply, Mr. Hugo Holloway was a man to watch out for.

The wine was exactly right, light and rather sharp. Laura was careful to drink only one glass. She had no way of forecasting what the day had in store, and it was no time for her to be sleepy. Looking around for cigarettes, she found some in a small gold box by the bed. Then it was time for the serious business of what to wear. In the ordinary way, Laura had few problems of selection. She would hunt until she found something that suited her, rejecting everything on the way, without difficulty. The situation here was different. Here she had to decide, not which to accept, but which she could reject, a matter that was to take all her concentration.

Downstairs Holloway sat facing Nagumi and Mike.

"This is a bad business," he said thoughtfully. "Not only have you two broken a fundamental rule, but you've also put me in a very difficult position."

"There was no alternative," returned Mike calmly.

"You could have left her to die," stated Holloway flatly.

Nagumi and Mike looked at each other uncomfortably, but made no reply.

"I mean, what kind of people are you?" demanded the producer. "You know perfectly well what's involved here. The lives of dozens of people could be put at risk through this girl. Thing of the capital tied up in our operation, the security we have to operate day and night. To say nothing of my personal position. Here I am, with a cover the organization has built up painstakingly over the years. And you calmly fly in some raw recruit who could tear the whole thing to shreds. And now you dump the problem on me."

He was perfectly right, as the others acknowledged privately.

"You can blame me, if you wish," said Nagumi quietly. "I have done always exactly what the Council instructed. But I have never been asked to murder an innocent woman, and I couldn't bring myself to do it."

171

"Me neither," chimed in Mike.

"Sentimental crap," snapped Holloway.

He tapped irritably at the table top with thick fingers.

"It's no good," he announced, "I just can't take this on myself. I'll have to contact other people. Kish-Kish will rustle up some grub, and I hope you enjoy it. It's not too late to do something about this girl, and if that's the way the vote goes, you two are elected for the job."

He went out of the room, and the two men watched his retreating back. Mike broke the silence first.

"Great," he said bitterly. "Just great."

Nagumi shrugged.

"I shall not enjoy the job any more than you Mike, if we have to do it. But you know yourself that Hugo is right. We can't afford to be soft about this. It could be the girl or the whole operation."

"All right, all right, I've heard the sermon once. Just don't ask me to like it."

The tall Arab appeared, carrying a tray of food.

"You eat now," he indicated.

172

"I'm not hungry," they both said at once.

"Then perhaps a little wine."

The impassive Kish-Kish poured out two goblets full of wine, and handed one to each. They sipped glumly, and resumed staring at the floor.

Upstairs, Laura was admiring herself in her fourth final choice, and even now was tempted to try just one more dress. But she felt there was no point in it. Everything suited her to perfection, and this particular one, a crisp lime-green linen affair, seemed to have been moulded on to her. Yes, this was the one. Now for the hair.

"He's taking a hell of a time," grumbled Mike. "I thought our new radio guaranteed instantaneous contact."

"So it does," asserted Nagumi. "The contact is nothing. It is the ensuing conversation which is of consequence to us. I am hoping Hugo is talking us out of a particularly distasteful assignment. If so, he can be as long as he likes, so far as I personally am concerned."

The minutes dragged by. The men sat

with barely touched glasses in their hands, the tray of food ignored.

Deep in a fortified cellar of the house, Holloway spoke rapidly into a microphone, words that were being heard carefully in four different parts of the world.

In her room, Laura was giving a final touch to the shimmering copper hair. Now to give her fellow criminals a view of something rather more interesting than the overalled companion they were used to. But when she tried to open the door, she found it locked. Her first reaction was one of fear, but this was dismissed quickly by her ever present logic. After all, she was very much the new recruit. These men undoubtedly had things to discuss, things they would not wish her to hear.

She was quite right of course, but her confidence would have nose-dived if she had any inkling of the nature of their conversation.

Mike was busy with his private thoughts. The whole situation struck him as monstrously ironic. He'd spent months tracking down the killer of his friend John. After carrying out a perfectly justified execution, he found himself in jail. To be rescued from there by anyone put him seriously in that person's debt. But to have that person prove to be John's widow only involved him more personally than ever. And now, to be sitting here, waiting for possible instructions to eliminate her, it was more than any one man should be expected to do.

Nagumi watched him covertly. The astute Japanese had a good idea of what was going on in the other man's mind, and he had every sympathy with him. But there would be no hesitation from Mike if the decision went against them. He, Nagumi, would see to that. The organization was ruthless in cases of disobedience, and Mike was too good a man to lose.

The thoughts of both of them were interrupted by footsteps in the hall. Hugo Holloway came through the door, and stood staring at them.

"Well?" demanded Mike.

"It was not an easy decision," returned

Holloway slowly. "There was a good deal of back and forth among us. I stressed your good records as much as I could. Also the fact that she was John's widow."

He paused heavily, and the only sound was the nervous tapping of Nagumi's fingers at the side of his glass.

"Hugo, for God's sake, what is the verdict?" Mike blurted out.

"The lady stays. It seems we have a new recruit."

10

Late that night, Laura let herself into her flat. She noted the half pint of milk, waiting outside the door, and picked it up as she went through. There were a few letters on the mat, and these she bent to gather, pushing the door shut with her foot. Going through to the kitchen, she switched on the light, and set about making some tea. Five minutes later she was sitting in the small lounge, sipping tea and enjoying a cigarette. A very clear-headed person normally, she was nevertheless having difficulty in adjusting her mind to the extraordinary chain of events of — was it only the past two days? As things happened she went along from one stage to the next, carried along by the excitement, the sheer improbability of it all. Now, finding herself suddenly back among calm and order, it was hard to adjust her mind to the fact that those things had really happened. Almost unconsciously, she pulled up her sleeve, and there was no escaping the slight tan she had taken from those few hours in Morocco. And the clothes, they too were real, and certainly not hers. She touched the arm of the chair, feeling its solidity, its fixed place in the scheme of things. This was her home. This had no part of jail-breaks, helicopters and pistols. And yet she knew nothing would ever really be the same again. This would remain her anchorage, but beyond the door was another world. Not her familiar, fairly tight world of work and friends. This was a strange unpredictable world, full of danger and excitement. A faint flush came into her face, as she recalled how her blood had raced so often in the past hours. She hadn't felt anything like it for a very long time. They had said she would be hearing from them again, that they now regarded her as one of themselves. Secretly, she was rather proud of their acceptance.

Remembering the letters, she picked them up and sorted quickly. There was one with French stamps on it, and this she opened first, puzzled. As she unfolded the typed sheets, she remembered what the masked man had told her. The letter was from the House of Charpentier. She was offered a nominal retainer of five hundred a year to report on any interesting local wines she may encounter on her travels. If, as a result, any trade developed, Laura would be paid six and a quarter per cent commission. There was a whole page on the particular qualities which would interest them. It was important however, not to waste their time merely in order to demonstrate that she was doing something to earn her retainer. They were quite content to await her considered selections, and the retainer would be permanent.

Not bad, she mused. Ten pounds a week for doing nothing at all, if she didn't choose. It was as good as a pension. There was also a small carte d'identité, with gold crusted edges, which established her as an authentic representative of the ancient House.

There was also a letter from her agent. A film company had shown some interest in *The Angled Horizon* and if anything came of it he would be in touch at once. The other envelopes contained bills, except a statement from her bank, which told her she need have no immediate fears of penury.

Laura found herself yawning, which was hardly surprising, when she recalled how long it had been since she slept. She went out into the kitchen, and was pouring a final cup of tea when there was a ring at the doorbell. A glance at her watch showed the time as ten minutes to midnight, hardly a normal hour for callers. Puzzled, she went to the door, attached the sliding chain, and opened it. A tall smooth-faced man of about fifty bowed to her.

"Mrs. Kilburn?"

"Yes. What can I do for you?"

"I'm a police officer, madam. I wonder if you could spare me a few minutes?"

"Police? Whatever for? And do you know what time it is? Can't you come at a more reasonable time?"

He nodded seriously.

"I have madam. This is my fourth call

today. You have not been at home."

She was torn between a desire to shut the door, and an intense curiosity to know what it was all about.

"How do I know you're not a burglar? Anybody can call himself a policeman."

He extended his hand, holding a small leather card case. It told her he was Detective Superintendent Bruce, of U Branch, New Scotland Yard. There was a passport size photograph of him pasted in the centre.

"H'm. Oh well, I suppose you can come in."

"Thank you."

She closed the door, released the chain, and opened it wide. He came in slowly, as if anxious not to alarm her.

"In here."

She took him into the lounge, and asked him to sit down. His keen eyes took in the room, and she felt certain he could draw the whole place from memory.

"Well, Superintendent, what is this all about? It must be terribly important if you've been here four times. Do you want to see my car insurance or something?"

He smiled faintly, shaking his head.

"No madam, I'm sure it's quite in order. Things of that kind are not dealt with by my department, in any case."

"Oh yes, U Branch. I don't believe I've heard of that."

"Good. We like to think we operate with the minimum of fuss. We deal with odd situations. In fact, the U stands for Unusual. Anything which doesn't fall squarely within one of the regular departments is passed on to us."

Laura laughed, wishing she felt as light-hearted as she sounded.

"Then I'm afraid you have the wrong woman. Believe me, I'm a very ordinary sort of person. Nothing unusual here."

"Perhaps."

He had an infuriating way of speaking very slowly, as if anxious that every word should be thoroughly masticated by the listener.

"Some odd things have been happening, Mrs. Kilburn. I wondered whether you might be able to throw some light on them. To begin with, and please forgive my mentioning what I'm sure must be a painful subject, there was the very unfortunate death of your husband."

She felt herself suddenly become icy calm. The next few minutes were going to be extremely difficult.

"I'm afraid I don't understand you. John was killed in a car crash, as I'm sure you must know. It's a subject I try not to think about, much less discuss."

He nodded, and she thought there was a touch of sympathy in his manner.

"Believe me, I would not refer to it, unless it were necessary. At the time it seemed a straightforward matter, and not something in which my department would have any involvement. There was, however, another branch which had been taking a mild interest in your husband for some time before his death."

Laura had risen now, white-faced.

"If you have come here to slander my husband, you had better get out now. And you had better consult your legal experts first thing in the morning, because I won't let this rest."

Superintendent Bruce did not seem at all taken aback at this outburst, but nodded slightly as though expecting something of the kind.

"Please hear me out, Mrs. Kilburn. Perhaps what I say later will enable you to look on me more kindly."

Slowly, anger still in her eyes, she sat down.

"On learning of your husband's accident, this other branch thought a few routine enquiries were called for. It transpired that there had been another man staying at the same mountain hotel with your husband. An American by the name of Monahan. Is that name familiar to you?"

Laura shook her head.

"No. I don't remember any friend of John's by that name. There could be some mistake of course."

Bruce looked at her quizzically.

"It is always a possibility," he admitted. "But I am not used to receiving inaccurate information from these particular people. However, there was no sign of Monahan after the accident. Then a little while later, a man was drowned in the Solent, an Englishman whom we happened to know was involved in gun-running and drug-smuggling among other things."

"I'm afraid I don't see any connection," Laura contributed.

"I hope to provide one. A few weeks ago, another man was killed. This time it was what appeared to be a drunken brawl, in a little village not far from Marseilles. The police apprehended the murderer, and it was none other than Monahan. The dead man was a Frenchman, also a known criminal, and an occasional associate of the man who had drowned. Last night, the jail was broken into, and Monahan rescued."

He paused at this, and had a long look into Laura's impassive face. Her mind was racing, and she knew she had to act as she had never acted before if she was to deceive this man.

"I still don't see — "

"Please. The rescue was extremely well-planned and conducted. There was one party of people on foot. Their task was to ensure that the police were unable to get out of the jail. Then a second party arrived in a helicopter — " he paused on that word and looked over at Laura — "who proceeded to lift out the bars of Monahan's cell, using the helicopter as a kind of mobile winch. It was entirely successful. However, at one stage, one of the party on the ground was recognized by an officer inside the jail. He had spent several years with the Deuxième Bureau, and was at the jail overnight quite by chance. The man he recognized was one Emilio Bartello. The name is possibly familiar to you?"

Laura shook her head slowly.

"No, I don't know anyone by that name. Why should I?"

The superintendent didn't reply immediately to the question, but remained quite still, looking at her. Laura wished he wouldn't. Her intuition told her that this man was used to looking at people. Those eyes had a quality of their own, eyes which had looked at many people before, while the ears took in whatever the subject was saying.

"No reason, Mrs. Kilburn. An interesting chap, Bartello. He has been idling around the Mediterranean for some years now.

186

Always seems to have plenty of money, but no one seems to know where he gets it."

Before she could prevent herself, Laura blurted out:

"It sounds much more like a matter for the Inland Revenue."

"Perhaps. But one thing we do know about him. He was a friend of your late husband's."

The room was very quiet. Laura had difficulty in restraining her fingers from twiddling.

"I really don't see how he could have been, without my knowledge. Or, even if he was, I don't see any significance in it."

"Really, Mrs. Kilburn? Then perhaps we should go on a little further. Let us think again of the Englishman and the Frenchman. Both known criminals and as I say, occasional associates. At the time of your husband's unfortunate death, these two were staying at another hotel, not ten miles from the one where your husband and the man Monahan were staying. Immediately following the accident, they moved out. In fact, they did more than that. They disappeared from sight completely. Then they died. First the Englishman, later the Frenchman. And it was Monahan who killed the Frenchman. Monahan, a friend of your husband's. Monahan was rescued from prison by helicopter. One of the people involved in that rescue was Bartello, also a friend of your husband's. Does this chain of events suggest anything to you Mrs. Kilburn?"

"I don't even see it as a chain of events," she returned calmly. "To me it is only a series of incidents which you seem to imagine connect up in some way."

"You may be right," he conceded. "We policemen are all alike. We like answers you know. We like logic, and sequence, and answers."

She smiled at him in an amused fashion.

"And what answer do you derive from this particular logical sequence?"

He did not answer at once, but regarded her with some care. Then he changed the subject.

"Have you ever heard of an organization

called Revenge Incorporated?"

The puzzlement on her face this time was genuine.

"No. It sounds like a television series."

His face cracked into an easy grin.

"Do you know, that's exactly what I have said, once or twice. But whatever views one has regarding television series, they are for amusement only, as the pinball machine people say. Revenge Incorporated, regrettably, is not."

"It may sound rather stupid of me, but I'm afraid I haven't the vaguest idea of what you're talking about."

"No? Well, I don't know very much about it myself. The little I do know has taken many police forces several years to piece together. It seems there is a band of people, people of wealth and resource, who are not satisfied with the normal legal proceedings for administering justice. They take the law into their own hands. I could cite you a number of quite extraordinary incidents, in many different parts of the world, where these people have appeared suddenly, carried out some coup, usually

189

with unpleasant results for some criminal or other, and then disappeared."

"I would have thought they were public benefactors," Laura said.

"Would you? I'm afraid I cannot indulge in such romantics. The plain fact is these people are themselves criminals. They have no regard for the law, and they have even killed on occasion. Oh no, there is nothing beneficial about the organization."

"You know, superintendent, I really am beginning to wonder where all this is getting us," Laura interrupted. "You march in here, come out with all these extraordinary allegations, then tell me a tale about some secret society. What is the point of it all please? I really am rather tired."

The penetrating eyes flicked over her.

"You've no idea?"

"None," she said firmly.

"Very well. I should tell you at the outset that I am rather an unusual kind of policeman. We are all expected to be, according to the public and the popular press, rather stodgy, dreary creatures.

Unimaginative plodders. In my thirty years of service I have indeed met one or two people who merit that description. About the same percentage, I would estimate, as one would find in insurance, banking or any other of the — um — less adventurous jobs. However, the people of U Branch are quite a different kettle of policemen. They are selected for their highly developed imaginations, their intuition, their willingness to look outside the ordinary run."

"How about conceit?" Laura blurted out the question, before she could prevent herself.

The superintendent was not remotely put out, or if he was, he gave no sign. Instead he smiled, a gentle pleasant smile.

"Why yes, that too, if one is to be honest. Nevertheless, we achieve results of sufficient merit for the authorities to retain the department. Now I will tell you what I think Mrs. Kilburn. This organization, with its paperback title, Revenge Incorporated, is not quite the closed book to me that it was originally.

Over the years, I have learned things about it. About its people, about its methods. Oh, not as much as I should have liked, I admit that freely. But at least it is now more to me than a mere name. I believe your husband was a member."

He waited after he said it as though in anticipation of a further outburst. But Laura sat quite still, achieving now that icy calm for which she had been striving. Bruce, seeing her composure continued.

"I also believe, your husband had become known as a person who had taken part in some enterprise or other, sponsored by Revenge Incorporated. The people who had suffered by his efforts killed him, or rather, had him killed. Those responsible were the French and English criminals I mentioned. I think the man Monahan acted in retaliation, killing both. Certainly, there is no question but that he killed the man in France."

Laura felt it was safe to speak now.

"You are right about one thing at least."

He looked at her expectantly.

"Really? It would be interesting to know what."

"Your imagination," she returned coolly. "It certainly is highly developed."

"There is more to come. I also believe this organization has been in contact with you, and that you were the person who flew that helicopter."

Laura laughed now. To her relief, it sounded quite natural.

"Well, superintendent, I have no answer to that. I'm afraid you've really taken the wind out of my sails this time."

"You deny it then?"

"Deny it?" she echoed incredulously. "Why my dear man, it's the most preposterous rubbish I think I've ever heard."

"I have of course made mistakes in the past," he admitted.

"I can well believe it," she assured him. "In fact, I would guess your mistakes average is on the high side."

"But not this time, I believe," he said matter-of-factly. "Oh, by the way, may I see your passport?"

"If I can find it."

She was glad of the excuse to get up and move around. She knew exactly where her passport was but nevertheless spent five full minutes of drawer opening and searching before she produced it.

"Ah, here it is. I don't think you'll find anything in there about visits to France lately."

"I don't expect to," he returned, flicking over the pages. "These people are not over-nice about small formalities of this kind. Thank you."

He handed the small booklet back, and Laura replaced it in a drawer.

"I don't think there is a great deal of point in prolonging this, Mrs. Kilburn. You obviously are not going to tell me anything, so I must proceed on the assumption that we are now on opposite sides."

"Sides?" she repeated.

"Of the law. Make no mistake, what these people are doing is criminal. Those who work with or for them are also criminals. It's all very well to deceive oneself with a lot of high flown chatter about righting the wrongs of the world. There is only one law-enforcement agency in this country. I represent that authority. Please think about it. A telephone call to New Scotland Yard will reach me eventually. I bid you goodnight."

She walked with him to the door. As he left he said, almost as an afterthought:

"Oh, and by the way, don't plan on any trips abroad for a while. I think you might find officialdom just a little awkward about giving permission. Goodnight."

She closed the door slowly behind him, vaguely depressed to be regarded as an enemy by such an obviously wise and pleasant person. Still, she reminded herself, she wasn't a child, and she'd known perfectly well what she was doing.

"What you need my girl, is a good night's sleep."

11

She woke late, fully refreshed. As she set the percolator to work, she was thinking about the superintendent's visit, and at the distance of a night's rest, found it not nearly so depressing. Even more cheering was the morning mail. There was an offer for paperback rights of *Tall in the Sky* for Norway, Sweden and Denmark. A second letter was from a feminist association inviting her to address a luncheon. She wasn't looking forward to that one at all, picturing, at once, those rows of exotic hats, and the faintly hostile atmosphere as she rose to her feet. But, it all helped the sales.

As she sat sipping at the strong coffee, Laura experienced her usual feeling of guilty pleasure. It was wrong, she always felt, for a healthy young woman to be sitting around idle at ten in the morning, while outside the world was at work. She had never fully accustomed herself to the freedom from routine her writing had brought her. The fact that she frequently worked late at night, while the rest of the world was at play, never quite compensated for the freedom of the mornings.

To rid herself of the feeling, she sat down at her typewriter, determined to work herself into a state of grace. At the end of an hour and a half, her total effort had produced one and a half sheets of quarto. As she read it for the tenth time, she realized it was rubbish. With a sigh, she crumpled up the work and threw it in the waste-paper basket. It was going to be one of those days. Hardly surprising, after the excitement of the previous forty-eight hours. It was no day for sitting around alone. Today, she had to do something positive, something physical. Half an hour later, she parked outside Tony's Gym. A tall blond young man smiled cheerfully when he saw who it was.

"Hallo, Mrs. Kilburn. Haven't seen you for weeks."

"I've been busy, Tony. Anybody here I can have a bout with?"

He reflected on this for a moment, then shook his head.

"Sorry. Only a few ladies in today. Mostly the keep fit type, I'm afraid. Nobody able to fight up to your standards."

"Oh." She was disappointed. "I suppose you're all booked up?"

"No. Matter of fact I had a cancellation this morning. Lady caught mumps. I can give you" — he looked at his watch — "twenty minutes if you like."

"Fine. I'll get ready."

She was out of the changing room in record time. Tony eyed her appreciatively. Why anyone who looked like Laura Kilburn should want to bother to exert herself was always a mystery to him.

"You don't need any exercise," he told her. "Why don't you just walk around outside? Be wonderful publicity for the place."

She grinned. She liked Tony, with his easy informality.

"Enough of your old flannel, me lad," she remonstrated. "Let's go and toss each other around for a while."

They stood on the padded floor, sizing each other up. Tony knew her for a wily and resourceful opponent. Soon, he made a grab for her, catching nothing but air as she leaped nimbly to one side, kicking him adroitly behind the knee at the same time. That was the end of the friendly period. For the next fifteen minutes, they grappled and strained at each other, the woman giving as good as the man. Dropping backwards to the mat, Tony broke what had threatened to be a dangerous stranglehold, flinging Laura away from him in the same movement.

"Whoa," he called, as she began another spring at him. "Sorry, Mrs. Kilburn, that'll have to do. My next appointment is almost due."

She checked herself, nodding. They both stood breathing steadily and grinning at each other.

"That was good, Tony. Exactly what I needed. Thanks for fitting me in."

"Pleasure. I just hope you've left me enough steam to see me through the afternoon."

She showered quickly and got dressed.

Now she felt on top of the world. And hungry. As she prepared to leave, Tony excused himself from the stout woman who was making heavy weather of the lightest pair of dumbells in the place, and came across.

"Mrs. Kilburn, this may sound daft, but is anyone following you?"

She looked at him quickly.

"Following me? Not that I know of. Why would anyone want to do that?"

"I wouldn't know. But there's a bloke opposite in a blue Austin. He pulled in just after you arrived, and he's been sitting watching the entrance. Doesn't take his eyes off it. Could be my imagination I s'pose."

She looked across at the car. Behind the wheel sat a non-descript individual of about thirty. He was wearing a crumpled grey suit.

"I don't know him. Anyway, thanks for looking out for me, Tony. I'll be seeing you."

"So long Mrs. Kilburn. Take care of yourself."

He watched, puzzled, as she climbed

behind the wheel and moved off. At once, the blue Austin followed. He'd been right then. Funny business.

"Tony," complained his heavy apprentice.

"Coming," he replied.

In the driving mirror, Laura watched the blue Austin maintaining a steady twenty yards behind her. It could only mean one thing. Bruce was having her followed. Not that it mattered very much. She wasn't proposing to do anything illegal, and certainly she wasn't going to lead them to Revenge Incorporated. She wouldn't know how even if she wanted to. Nevertheless, she didn't relish the thought of having someone spying on her. Puzzling over what to do about it, she suddenly had an idea and smiled to herself in the rear mirror. She drove around the streets until she saw a police constable strolling steadily round his beat. Pulling into the nearest available space, she left the car and approached him.

"Officer, please help me. There's a man following me."

The constable's eyes swiftly scrutinized the street.

"Which one, miss?"

"Oh, not a pedestrian. He's in a car. That blue Austin down there."

He looked towards the spot where the blue Austin was parked.

"Are you sure, miss? Why would he do that?"

The policeman was trying to keep scepticism from his voice. He'd heard this one before, many times. But, he admitted to himself, mostly from old ladies or others searching for some romantic fulfilment. This girl would have no need of any such fantasies. Her husband perhaps, or a jealous boy friend.

"He doesn't seem to be doing any harm, miss. Just sitting there reading his paper. Are you sure you couldn't be mistaken?"

Intuitively, Laura knew she mustn't overplay her hand.

"Well," she began doubtfully, "it's possible I suppose. But he's been everywhere I've been, all day. It could just be coincidence, but it's beginning to frighten me. I want to go home, but I'm certainly not going to lead him there. Couldn't you just speak to him, please? I'll apologize to him if I'm wrong."

Sensible, decided the constable. No hysterical female here. Yes, it could just be possible she was right.

"Very well miss. You just wait here, and I'll have a word with him."

He walked easily down to the parked car, and tapped on the window. The driver looked up, rolled the window down.

"Excuse me sir, but there's a young lady down the street who seems to think you're following her."

Laura watched the conversation begin, got back into her car and drove quickly away.

"She's right. I am. U Branch. Look out man, she's getting away."

"Hold on."

The constable was no longer detached.

"You must have some identification."

The driver sighed, and with a resigned expression, reached into his jacket as Laura's car disappeared round the corner.

"Satisfied?"

"Very sorry sergeant," said the constable. "But you can see my position. If everybody who wanted to chase young women just said he was from U Branch, we'd be in a fine state."

The driver nodded. The constable was right of course. But the few seconds it took him to identify himself was sufficient time for Mrs. Kilburn to get lost in the traffic. And would be, he acknowledged glumly, the next time.

Laura waiting at some traffic lights, thought suddenly of the scene, when the discomfited man who had been set to follow her had to explain to the superintendent that he'd been prevented by a policeman. Unable to prevent a sudden laugh, she stopped abruptly at the sight of the leering fat man who had pulled up beside her at the lights.

An hour later, having disposed of a substantial meal accompanied by half a bottle of a very reasonable Beaune, she went into a cinema in Leicester Square and settled to the enjoyable prospect of watching James Stewart put the West to rights. A passion for the Western was something she'd acquired from John, and many a time in the past they had travelled half across London to catch up on some old favourite. It was early evening when she left the cinema, comfortably assured that the Iroquois would not be causing any further problems for a while.

She wandered aimlessly along Coventry Street. The crowds were quite thick now, toils of the day behind them, and bent on making the most of the evening ahead. For Laura, that was a problem. In her case, there was no evening ahead, only the prospect of long hours alone in the flat. Lately, she had become so accustomed to the empty period between afternoon and morning that it was more or less routine. Now that she had been lifted out of that routine in no uncertain manner, she viewed the night ahead with more resentment than usual. She could go out, of course. It was no social crime any longer for a woman to appear at a theatre or a concert unaccompanied. But it always felt wrong somehow. People always took more than a passing interest in the beautiful girl who sat alone. And of course there would be the predators, the helpful males who would open the doors, light her cigarettes uninvited and generally make themselves a nuisance.

"Miss. Miss. 'Scuse me miss."

Someone tugged at her elbow, and she looked round into the worried face of a boy no more than twelve years old.

"You dropped this, miss."

He held out an envelope, and she took it automatically.

"No, it wasn't me — " she began, but the boy was gone, scuttling away like a rabbit from a cornfield.

Laura turned the envelope slowly and there was no doubt it belonged to her. There in large square capitals she read 'Mrs. Laura Kilburn'. Ripping it open, she extracted the sheet of paper inside and unfolded it. The same large capitals told her to ring a Strand number, adding 'Use call box.' She tingled with excitement. There was no doubt who the message was from, and the evening took on a new colour. Impatiently, she waited outside the familiar red box, while the young man inside gave a soundless performance of trying to persuade whoever it was at the other end. To judge by his facial expressions, and the liberal employment of his spare hand, he wasn't doing very well. It was minutes before he emerged, defeated finally, and wandered disconsolately away.

Laura entered the box and dialled. The receiver was lifted instantly.

"Mrs. Kilburn?"

"Yes," she replied.

The voice at the other end was male, rich and plummy.

"I think you might have an inkling as to who this is? We had the pleasure of your company recently."

"I haven't forgotten. Do you want to see me?"

"Yes, dear lady. Something has cropped up unexpectedly. It seems that your — um — special qualifications might be most helpful to us again. Would you be interested?"

"Very definitely, yes. What do you want me to do?"

"We should like you to come right away. Your flat is being watched, as you may know. At the moment you are quite safe, but if you go home you may not be so lucky next time. Do you know the Coypu?"

The Coypu. No, that was a new one. "I'm afraid not."

"Very well. It's in Old Compton Street. The taxi driver will know. I will meet you there."

"How will I know you?"

"I shall be the only man there who knows *you* Mrs. Kilburn. Shall we say fifteen minutes? There is a bar just inside the entrance."

"Yes, I'll be there."

Outside she was lucky to get a taxi immediately.

"Coypu miss? Oh yes, I know it. New place. Right hand side from this end."

Theatre traffic had thinned out, and five minutes after putting down the telephone, Laura stood outside the Coypu. It looked no better and no worse than most, except for the rather unpleasant model of the rat-like creature after which the place was named. Inside, it was pleasant. Soft new carpets, and quiet lighting. Laura did not go into the bar. Instead she headed straight through the door marked 'Her', to repair the ravages of the day before putting in her appearance.

When she emerged, she pushed open the glass door to the bar and went in, standing for a moment in the doorway. There were not many people inside, and she could not tell which of the several men was waiting for her. To judge by their faces, they all were. But only one had any claim, and he came forward now, arms outstretched.

"Mrs. Kilburn, how nice."

He was medium height, slightly tubby, with an open cheerful face of the kind that made people respond automatically. Laura felt herself put out both hands for him to take, and he clasped them briefly.

"I was afraid you might not be able to come."

"Oh yes. I've been looking forward to it."

His grin broadened as she followed his cue. The rest of the people in the bar lost interest. The girl had arrived, been inspected, and claimed. Now she was one of them. Next, please.

He led her to a small table at one side of the room, on which stood the remnants of a large brandy. A half-smoked cigar rested in the diminutive ashtray.

"What can I get you to drink?"

"Could I have some gin please. Tonic and ice."

"Of course."

He was back quickly, presenting her drink with a small flourish. Then sitting down, he produced a thick gold case, flicking it open.

"Do you care for these?"

She reached out, then saw the case contained small cheroots.

"Oh, no thank you, I don't smoke those."

"Capital."

He shrugged at the case, and the cheroots lifted over to reveal a row of cigarettes beneath. This time she took one. Her escort nodded as though pleased, and lit the cigarette from a chunky gold lighter in his other hand.

"My information is always first class," he told her confidentially, "but I'm one of those people who has to check for himself. You don't mind?"

Laura sipped at her drink, looking at him.

"It's difficult to answer that, since I haven't the remotest idea what you're talking about."

He beamed at this. She thought he was really one of the most cheerful and benign creatures she'd met.

"Well, I know our people are careful, to put it mildly. But I like to satisfy myself about — er — newcomers."

"Oh. And how do I seem to be doing?"

She was not, to her surprise, offended.

"Splendidly. Oh I do assure you, splendidly. It's my own little selection procedure. Really totally unnecessary in your case, in the light of recent — um — developments. But life is such an uncertain proposition, that I'm always just a mite reserved about new people. You understand?"

"I don't blame you. In the light of

recent — um — developments, I can see that there could be times when it might be precarious to pick a wrong 'un."

She grinned as she mimicked his tone, and he responded with a wide smile.

"And a sense of humour, too. Really, this promises to be quite delightful. Have you read *Le Figaro* lately, incidentally?"

Puzzled by the question for a moment, she suddenly realized what he meant.

"No," she admitted. "That was silly of me, but I didn't think of it."

"Oh, there's some very interesting stuff in there, I do assure you. In that one, there is a graphic account of the whole business. Rather too accurate in spots for comfort."

"Oh?" she looked up. "Does that mean there are going to be any complications?"

"That is very doubtful," he assured her. "But it is always unwise to underestimate the French police. They are very good indeed. It is a mistake made by many people. Never, I am thankful to say, by our little group of friends. No, you need have no fears."

He raised his glass to her, eyes

twinkling, as he sipped sparingly at his brandy. Now Laura knew where it was she'd seen the face before. This man was the prototype of Happy, the cheerful dwarf in Snow White. That was it, Happy.

"Mrs. Kilburn, there is a little diversion which I think you will find interesting. We can't discuss it here, naturally, as some of our other friends are waiting to meet you. I thought, if it is agreeable to you, we would have just one drink here, then go and join them?"

"Of course."

She finished her drink and stubbed out the cigarette.

"Ready when you are."

He rose at once, and she noted again how graceful he was in his movements, despite the bulky build.

"I have a car quite near. You know this parking business really is getting out of hand these days."

He took her arm, and led her out of the place, chattering amiably. At the bar, a dark-haired man took some money from his pocket and left it on the counter.

12

Happy drove expertly north out of London. Laura hadn't travelled that way for years, and was quite content to stare out of the windows, noting all the changes that had taken place. As though reading her mind he said:

"Do you know this part?"

"I used to, but it's years since I was here."

"Used to be lovely," he said regretfully. "Even ten or twelve years ago, it was still very pleasant. Look at it now. All these blasted supermarkets and housing estates. They'll have the whole country covered in concrete in another twenty years. Ah this is us."

He turned off the main road, on to a narrow lane where the tall hedgerows linked overhead. Drawing into the bank, he stopped the car.

"I'm very sorry about this dear lady, but would you mind?"

He handed her a silk scarf. "Just normal security, you understand."

She took it without question and tied it round her head, being very careful to be certain she could not see.

"Awful bore really, and I'm sure quite unnecessary in your case."

The car pulled smoothly away again. Now that she was unable to see anything, the gentle motion of the ride began to make Laura quite drowsy. She had no idea of time or direction, and had to shake her head sharply as she realized he was speaking again.

" — quite comfortable. Hang on a moment, and I'll open the door."

Then she felt his hand on her arm, and she climbed out.

"Two steps up here. That's it. Duck your head, this is a low arch."

Her feet scrunched on gravel, then a door opened and they were inside. Hands undid the scarf, and she blinked in the sudden light.

"There now, that's better. You know, all the years I've been in this business, and all this stuff still makes me feel as though I'm playing games at school. Well now, here we are. Let me get you something."

It was a long low room, sparsely furnished. Judging by the fireplace, the house was probably very old.

"No, nothing for me, thanks."

"Then we can get down to business right away. I'll get the others in."

He pulled at a gold-tasselled rope. Far off, Laura thought she heard the faint sound of a bell. She was eager to ask questions, but she knew by now enough of the organization to be aware that questions were unwelcome. Still, she reflected with quiet relish, it was quite exciting that she could be halfway across the world this time tomorrow. She wondered whether here too, there might be a black helicopter perched on the roof. As the thought came into her mind she looked up automatically.

"Ah yes, the chandelier," beamed her host. "What good taste you have Mrs. Kilburn. I am told it was brought here originally from Spain in the mid-seventeenth century."

She nodded vaguely. The door opened and two men came in. One was short and compact, and quite the best-dressed man she'd ever laid eyes on. Looming behind him was an immense figure. He must have stood close to seven feet in height, and was broad like an ox. His skin was pale olive in colour, and the bald head gleamed dully from the subdued lighting in the room.

"Ah, there you are. Now our little party is complete. As you see gentlemen, Mrs. Kilburn has joined us. Mrs. Kilburn, may I present Leo," he pointed to the short man, who lowered his head gracefully, "and Kul. Kul, I fear is unable to greet you, as regrettably he lost his tongue in an incident many years ago."

The giant stared at her impassively, and Laura felt a quick, irrational fear.

"I am aware, naturally, that I have not introduced myself," went on the tubby man, "but I regret that circumstances do not permit it. Now Mrs. Kilburn, to business."

He lit a cigarette without proffering the case. Inhaling mightily, he treated Laura to one of his enormous beams. The others made no attempt to sit down.

"I take it there is no question but that you are willing to help us?"

The question surprised Laura.

"Why, of course. Is it necessary to ask?"

The beautifully dressed man looked quickly at her genial host.

"Does she know?"

His voice was clipped and faintly foreign.

"What is there to know?" demanded Laura. "I think I can say I have done everything that's been asked of me so far."

"Please, dear lady, do not excite yourself. I am sure your — um — performance has been more than adequate. That is not exactly what Leo meant."

He permitted himself a fat chuckle. Laura waited patiently while he enjoyed his private joke.

"No my dear, not quite what he meant at all. Mrs. Kilburn, I'm afraid I have not been completely frank with you. Yes, I think I must say it. Not entirely honest at all."

It seemed to the watching Laura that some of the good humour had left his face.

"Honest in what way?" she queried.

"Well now, you have made certain assumptions, and it is to my eternal discredit that I did not correct them. The fact is, although our interests are mutual, they are so for different reasons."

"Different reasons," echoed Laura uncomprehendingly.

"Quite. You see, taking this little matter in France the other evening. Not to put too fine a point on it, dear lady, I'm afraid our interests were in conflict on that occasion. Indeed, it was we here present, together with other — um — interested parties, who had the man Monahan placed in custody. In a round-about way."

"You mean that you are nothing to do with — with us," Laura hastily altered what she had been intending to say.

"On the contrary," he protested, "we all have a great deal to do with you.

Over the years, I may say, a great deal too much to do with you. But now, as always, our interests are in conflict. In brief madam, we represent the opposition."

Laura heard this dully. There was a sudden silence in the room, an oppressive cloying silence, or so it seemed. She looked from the smirking fat man to the dapper unsmiling Leo, and from him to the motionless Kul. She made a creditable effort to sound matter of fact.

"I see. And what do you want with me?"

There was no humour on the fat face now.

"They have recruited well, as always. However, I hardly expected emotion at this early stage. Now, Mrs. Kilburn, I am a realist. I know that you are a recent recruit, and it is not part of the induction procedure that you be permitted to learn very much. Where are you going?"

He snapped out the last words as Laura rose to her feet. Kul shifted his stance very slightly.

"Since you are obviously aware that I

know nothing, there seems to be little point in my remaining," Laura said calmly.

"Good. Oh yes, very good. Nevertheless, it will not do. Sit down."

All three men waited to see what she would do. She shrugged and returned to her seat.

"You underestimate yourself, Mrs. Kilburn. There must be certain things you have seen, certain faces. It may not be much, but your people really are so very retiring, any scraps of information are always welcome."

"I shall tell you nothing."

For the first time a slow smile came over Leo's face. Laura noted this uneasily.

"Mrs. Kilburn," he said silkily, "you are mistaken. You most certainly are going to tell us everything. Everything we want to know. What you mean to say is, you will do so unwillingly. Of this I have no doubt. There is no question as to whether you are going to tell us. The only question is, how long will you last before you do."

He delivered all this through the smiling lips, as though they were discussing the weather. It was not so much the words he spoke, as the expression in the cold eyes, which sent the first warning shiver down Laura's spine.

"You will learn, my dear, that in such matters Leo is never wrong," the fat man assured her. "He has been persuading people for many years to disclose information. It is our normal experience that after an interview with Leo, people are begging us to accept information. I have only ever known him to fail on one occasion."

He looked at her for reaction. Laura stared at the floor.

"Yes, only once. The man regrettably died before he could help us."

Leo shrugged.

"I could not be blamed. No one told me the fool had a weak heart."

Well, if I'm going, I had better be on my way, decided Laura. She stood again. The fat man was an arm's length away. Leo over to her left. The monstrous Kul was behind him.

"I find this unproductive," she answered. "I'm leaving."

The fat man pointed a remonstrating finger.

"I think not. We may have to prevent it."

Laura inclined her head in mock resignation. The fat man chuckled. She seized his outstretched arm, bringing her feet up into his stomach as she flung herself backwards to the soft carpet. He was completely unprepared for the attack, and sailed over her to crash against the wall, where he lay inert. Laura scrambled quickly to her feet as Leo came for her, leaping like a cat. She waited until he was almost on her, then sprang sideways, chopping hard at his neck. The blow was mistimed and landed harmlessly on his shoulder. It was sufficient to unbalance him, and before he could recover, she dived at his legs, twisting hard at a knee. Leo screamed and went down close to where Laura had sprawled. There was no mistake this time as she knifed at the side of his neck. He went limp.

Two down, she thought quickly. One

to go. As she made to get to her feet, she felt herself grasped suddenly from behind, and lifted as though she were a paper parcel. Kul crushed her to him, and Laura kicked back violently and attempted to get her elbows into striking positions. Her kicking landed on what felt like steel plate. If it had any effect at all on the giant, it was not reflected in any lessening of that terrible grip. She felt herself losing strength, as the mighty encircling arms grew tighter. Dropping her head, she tried to bite him, but his flesh was just out of reach. She felt roaring now, in her ears, and a red glaze came over her eyes. Shaking her head, she tried to clear her vision, but the roaring became louder and she seemed to be vanishing into a red mist. After that she knew no more.

* * *

A long way off, Laura seemed to hear a voice. Drowsily she put up a hand to rub at her eyes, but the hand would not move.

"She's coming round."

A hand on her head, and an ungentle thumb pulled back her eyelid. Light seared her eyes and she jerked her head away.

"Ah Mrs. Kilburn, there you are."

It was the voice of the fat one. The one, she recalled bitterly, who'd reminded her of the happy dwarf. Well, at least, she'd given him something to be unhappy about.

"Kul."

At the soft command her hair was grabbed and her head forced back.

"Come dear lady, we have wasted enough time."

She opened her eyes in the direction of the hated voice. Opposite her, the fat one sat in a deep chair, an open box of chocolates resting beside him. Laura gloated at the sight of the silk scarf which had been put to use as an improvised sling for his left arm. Turning her eyes she saw the man Leo, standing beside a small table covered with an assortment of objects, which included two or three bottles and an array of what seemed to

225

be medical instruments. He returned her stare implacably. The giant was not on view, and must therefore be behind her.

All these things registered slowly, as she regained control of her senses. She found movement impossible, and realized that she was bound to the hard wooden chair. Her hands had been secured behind her back, and her feet splayed so as to contact the chair legs.

"You have been very foolish, my dear," purred Happy. "For a moment, I had been tempted to treat you as gently as possible realizing your amateur status in this matter. However, I am afraid your little display of temperament has removed you from the amateur ranks. Also, you have wasted more than an hour, which is quite unforgivable. You will be good enough to answer my questions without further delay."

Laura called him something which surprised even herself. He gave no sign of having heard her.

"I want a fully detailed description of how you were inducted into this group of yours. I want names and descriptions of every person you have contacted. Finally I want precise information on the ways in which you released the murderous Mr. Monahan. You may begin."

She stared at him with hatred. Her mind was in a turmoil. These people were going to hurt her, she had little doubt of that. What nagged at her was the fact that she couldn't quite grasp why she should bother herself to protect Revenge Incorporated. It was a ridiculous title anyway. After all, she hardly knew them. And surely she'd done enough for them already, helping to release a murderer, and placing herself well outside the law to help a man she'd never even met previously. It wasn't as though she owed them anything. And none could say she betrayed them lightly. She'd put up a pretty good fight, as the fat one's damaged arm testified. Was there one good reason why she should endure any pain, any further humiliation?

All these things flashed through her mind as she watched Leo delicately sorting through the items on the table. He picked up something, a long slender glass instrument and came towards her. She opened her mouth to say something and closed it abruptly. John. That was what she'd been searching for. If she hadn't been so confused, it would have come to her earlier. She was doing it for John. At once her mind was clear of any doubts or confusion. Her people were his people. They were his friends. These others, these animals, they were his enemies. Worse, they were the ones who took him away from her, murdered him. A great peace came over her now. These people couldn't touch her. Leo was beside her now leaning over. The glass thing was in his hand but out of sight behind her head. She felt the tip of it below her ear, a slight pain as the point pierced her flesh. Then the world exploded in an agony of red and white. A thin scream as from a tortured animal flowed from her lips.

"You will find Leo most proficient, I assure you. Many of his little practices are his own patent. Once more Leo."

Again the blinding pain streamed through her, seeming to flow right through her body. Laura doubted whether she could take very much more of it.

"Any time you are ready, Mrs. Kilburn."

She began to talk. A long rambling tale of how she met a man in a club in Knightsbridge. Laura had not written successful novels without being able to tell a convincing story.

"And where exactly on the coast was this boat moored?"

"I — I haven't any way of telling. I was blindfolded throughout the journey. But it was on the south-east coast."

"You lie, Mrs. Kilburn. It is most unfortunate. No, Leo."

Laura opened her eyes in time to see Leo standing back from her, the glass monstrosity in his hand. There was disappointment on his face.

"Now Leo," soothed the fat man, "I just don't want to spoil your little entertainment. There will be more, I promise." Turning to Laura he said conversationally, "You see, dear Leo is such an artist, he gets quite carried away. He tends to forget that this particular diversion sometimes causes irreparable brain damage. You must not misunderstand me. What happens to you is naturally of less than no consequence. But before it happens, I do require to have this information. Now Leo, if you please, something a little more refined."

The fat man sat back, drawing contentedly on his cigarette. Leo returned to the table, while Laura watched, hoping the desperate fear did not show in her eyes. The delicate hands raised a gleaming surgical knife, and Happy nodded approvingly.

"Yes, I think so. You know my dear, Leo learned his trade in the concentration camps during the last war. Some of his fellow countrymen had information which was needed to assist the war effort. They were quite remarkably difficult about parting with it, but Leo learned well. Indeed, he was held in some regard by the Gestapo."

She heard his voice only vaguely, her eyes transfixed by the shining steel as Leo approached. He bowed to her almost formally. When he spoke, it was as though addressing an audience of students.

"For this exercise, the medical profession insists on a general anaesthetic. It is the view of the leading professionals that although a local will be sufficient to ensure no pain, the visual shock to the patient is well above the normal toleration level. We shall of course have to dispense with any anaesthetic whatever."

The knife traced delicately around her middle. Laura braced herself against the awaited pain. There was a chuckle from the fat man.

"Really, you mustn't be so nervous. Leo is only preparing you. The man is an expert. You will not be hurt until he intends it."

The knife continued to move around her. Laura could hear the faint sound of slitting material, but amazingly the point of the blade made no contact with her flesh. Then there was a movement at her shoulders. Gently the top half of her dress slid from her and to the floor, where Leo kicked it aside. He held the knife close to her face for a moment while she stared at it in horrified fascination. Then, swiftly, he struck downwards. Again she clenched her teeth, but all she felt was her bra flying open as he severed it neatly.

"Ah."

There was a long intake of breath from the fat man. Laura flushed as she watched his eyes.

"What a pity," he breathed. "This kind of surgery is normally reserved for the most advanced cases of disease. It was never intended for this kind of sacrilege. However, it is your choice. Proceed."

He was no longer detached, but leaning forward excited, his eyes shining. Laura felt pain now, as the knife penetrated skin deep. She watched with terrified despair as the hair line left by the encircling blade spread slowly with thick bright blood. There was a crashing noise, and the knife stopped. Laura opened pain filled eyes, to see Leo fall back from her, blood welling from a dark hole in the immaculate shirt. She couldn't grasp what was going on. The fat man was on his feet, a large automatic in his hand. Two more crashes, and he fell awkwardly back as though someone had hit him. Now, into her vision came a wild figure dressed in the shining black overalls.

"Monahan," she muttered. "Oh Monahan."

"All right, me girl, the marines have landed. Where's that swine Kul?"

"I — oh — I thought he was in here."

"Hang on, mustn't spoil the party."

She was sobbing now, scalding tears spilling down her face as she sagged forward in the chair. Monahan nodded encouragement and went out of her view. There was shooting, outside, somewhere. Waves of oblivion swept over her, and she shook them off, only to give reality to the pain which seemed to be everywhere. There was a staccato rattle, as of machine gun fire. The door flew open, smashed from its hinges, and hung drunkenly askew. Framed in the opening was the massive Kul. In his hand glittered a huge curved knife. Laura struggled helplessly against the cruel ropes. Not like this, she protested. Not bound and naked in front of this leering pig. Kul stepped forward, his eyes opaque, and his knife extended well before him. She was afraid, God alone knew how afraid she was. But he would never know it. It became suddenly the most important thing in the world, that this torturing monstrosity would never have the satisfaction of knowing she was afraid at the last. Laura made a pitiable attempt to throw back her head. Then she spat at him. That much she could manage. He paused, as though disconcerted, then the knife moved slowly down towards her, its evil arc aimed at her breast. She watched with teeth clenched, fascinated as the light danced from the murderous point of the blade. It was going to miss. No, how could it. Yes, it was. And then she saw, as though watching a slow-motion film, the enormous knees buckle painfully under the mountainous Kul. He shook his head at her, as though trying to convey a message, held out his other hand as if to steady himself, then the great body shook. The gleaming head pitched towards her, and he lay face down at her feet, the knife useless beside his outstretched hand. Laura stared down at him unable to understand or believe what had happened. Until she saw his back. It was criss-crossed with ragged torn holes from which dark blood welled slowly.

"Are you all right, me dear?" The voice was quick with concern.

"Oh Monahan," she laughed weakly. "You do ask the silliest bloody questions."

13

People running, shouting, doors slamming. Laura stirred, groaned, felt quickly the soreness where the knife had left its mark. Her hands were free and with returning normality she crossed her arms quickly over her breasts. Then she realized someone had put a jacket on her, a man's jacket.

"We cannot remain, miss. Please, you will come now."

She found she was sitting on cold grass in the darkness. Looking up at the voice she saw a strange face. The accent told her he was foreign. Well, she'd had enough of strangers.

"Monahan," she said weakly. "Where?"

"He is waiting. Please, there is no time."

He helped her to her feet. Shock was wearing off rapidly, and she was feeling better with every step. The man walked solicitously beside her. There were cars lined up in the drive, lights on in several rooms of the house. And there, on the immaculate lawn, she could make out the familiar, heart-warming shape of the black helicopter. Laura almost wept.

"They gave you a bad time, didn't they?"

Monahan loomed suddenly from the darkness.

"Not too bad," she denied. "It was just as well you came when you did."

He laughed briefly.

"Thanks, Johann. I'll look after her. Will you help the others? I want to be out of here in precisely six minutes."

The other man disappeared into the house. The American held out a cigarette, already lit. Laura took it gratefully, feeling a quick pull where adhesive plaster had been placed over her cuts.

"I don't know what to say," she admitted. "How on earth did you find me?"

"That wasn't difficult. We've been sort of keeping an eye on you, ever since Detective Superintendent Bruce called. He's a clever devil, that one. We thought we ought at least to know what he was liable to find out."

"You mean you were spying on me?"

"Oh come on, you're not really complaining are you? After this?"

The beginnings of resentment were lost in her remorse.

"I'm — I'm sorry. Believe me."

"Forget it. Besides, we also had to watch out for this little bunch. They have an uncanny instinct for tracing new recruits. We like to be on hand to discourage too much fraternization."

"Frat — . With that ghastly crew? I suppose they're all — all — ?"

She left the question poised. Monahan nodded.

"Death was too merciful for them. We've had our little problems before, especially with Catlett. If you'd seen what happened to Johann's sister last year, you'd have realized how anxious we were to locate them again."

"Catlett?"

"Yes, the fat oily character. He's been quite a problem to us. When I got the description of the guy who contacted you,

I hardly dared hope it would be him."

"What will happen now? I mean, the police will be involved. Suppose they're able to connect me with this?"

Laura was remarkably calm now, discussing sudden death as if it were a matter of routine. She realized with shock how quickly she had become inured to violence and death.

"It is our view that the police in this country are overworked enough as it is. They have plenty of worthwhile crime to occupy their attention. We wouldn't want to have them running around in circles over a simple matter of de-licing like this. We won't bother them with it."

"And those men, the dead men?"

"Will be taken care of. The house is being stripped of anything we can use, money, passports, any information about our late friends and *their* friends. Then we shall burn it down. It's isolated, there isn't any question of harm coming to anyone else. And I'm afraid that's all the time we have, honey. Get into the second car, please. The black Ford."

Laura carefully trod out her cigarette

in the gravel drive, and did as Monahan had instructed. Through the window she watched the house. Flames appeared suddenly at an upper storey, then more at the opposite end of the house. From the front door, two men emerged, carrying bundles. They were followed quickly by three more. A low boom, and a sudden sheet of flame appeared on the ground floor, as near as Laura could guess, coming from the room where Catlett and the others had tortured her.

Now, another man came out by the front door, and lastly Monahan. He spoke to them all quickly and they dispersed to the waiting cars. Monahan came across to the Ford and climbed in beside her.

"Not bad," he said cheerfully. "Close to twenty thousand dollars in Italian lire, and three thousand in Chinese yen. Not bad."

"Where are we going?"

Laura was suddenly very tired, and all she could concentrate her mind on was a hot bath and bed.

"Just a minute."

He was watching the house expectantly.

The fire had a good hold now, in half a dozen places. There didn't seem to Laura to be any point in watching. There was little prospect of the fire going out. There was a rumbling explosion, and half the top of the house seemed to errupt.

"That's it."

Monahan switched on the engine, and they rolled smoothly forward. The other cars were moving too.

"What about the chopper?" she queried.

"Those boys'll be the last to leave. They have — um — other work to do."

She didn't want any details about what the other work may be, and there was no more conversation until they reached the major road.

"Where are we going?" she again asked.

"I've been thinking about that. You'd better come with me. You can't very well go home in that state. Half your clothes are missing and you look a mess. Even Bruce could be forgiven for finding it all a trifle suspicious."

A mess, she thought indignantly. Well, how did he expect her to look? How would anybody look if they'd had to put up with what she had? Unconsciously, her hand strayed to her hair.

"There's a mirror on a swivel there."

She found it, pulled it towards her. Monahan was right. She did look a mess. Thinking about the reception she would get back at the flat if the urbane Bruce really was waiting, she couldn't help grinning.

"See what I mean?" mocked the American. "That Miss World title is not for you right now."

She could scarcely be cross with the man who'd just saved her life. All she said was "Is there a comb at your place?"

When they entered the outskirts of London, Monahan turned into a side road and drew in close to a telephone box.

"Have to report," he said briefly, and got out.

She watched him in the pale light from the box, a tall dark figure, speaking quickly and seriously nodding frequently as he made his report on the night's work. He was soon back, slamming the door, and they were moving again.

242

"Could I ask what reception you got?" she said tentatively.

"Later. I want to think."

In Knightsbridge, he drove down a tunnel under a large block of flats. There were numbered garages at the end. Monahan unlocked one, drove expertly in, and stopped.

"Home, sweet home. Let's go."

She climbed out, wondering briefly what the arrangement was supposed to be when they got upstairs, but was too exhausted to care much. He took her arm, leading her to a bank of lifts.

"Let's hope to God nobody sees us," he chaffed. "I have a reputation to maintain around here. You won't do a hell of a lot for it, looking this way."

The flat was better than she'd expected. Large and comfortable, and by no means the untidy mess bachelor places were popularly supposed to be.

"Sit down there," he ordered.

Meekly, she relaxed into the deep chair indicated. Monahan opened a door in the wall, produced a crystal decanter and poured out drinks into chunky tumblers.

"It's brandy, just what you need."

Laura sipped at it, feeling the warm glow spreading through her body. There were cigarettes in a sandalwood box. The American sat opposite, deep in thought. She thought it best not to interrupt him.

"The Council are worried," he said finally.

"The Council. What about?"

He must mean the inner circle, the policy makers of the organization.

"This business tonight. Naturally they're pleased things turned out the way they did. Catlett and the others dead at last, especially that horror Leo. None of our people hurt. A perfect score."

Nobody hurt indeed, she thought resentfully.

"Then what is there to worry about?"

"There's you, honey. On two counts. First, the fact they got on to you so fast. We have no way of knowing whether they passed that knowledge on to others. That could be bad, for you. All of us, possibly."

Laura could see that. The prospect of

encountering any more of the same kind was not at all inviting.

"You said two counts," she prompted. "What's the other?"

"You're not going to like this. It was the ease with which they picked you up. That would never have happened to a real operator."

Monahan was right. She didn't like it a bit.

"That's hardly fair," she protested. "I've had little or no training. What little I know about things only emphasizes in my own mind the total secrecy of everything. I'm treated like an apprentice, and fair enough, I accept that. But these people treated me exactly the way you would have. It was all so familiar, so authentic. If you think I'm easily picked up in a bar in the ordinary way, try it some time."

He held up a hand to quell the outburst.

"All right, all right. I told you you wouldn't care for it. The question is, what to do about you? We can't just let you go back to your own life. Not yet

245

anyway. If those guys did manage to tip off others, we'd have to play this whole scene over. And next time we might not be so lucky."

That made sense.

"Perhaps I could go for a holiday, stay away for a few weeks?" she suggested.

"It won't do. What we have to do is keep you missing to give us at least a chance of learning whether they're interested in you. And we have to use that time to train you, so you'll be better able to look after yourself, if and when you come back."

It sounded reasonable until he got to the last part.

"What do you mean by 'if and when'?"

He drained the last of his brandy, tapping his fingers musically against the glass.

"Sometimes our people do get spotted. Either somebody in opposition gets wise to them, or the police get a little too close. There's a man like Bruce in almost every police force in the world. They don't hold down their jobs by getting nothing done. They are some of the finest police minds in the game, and they know their business. The one in Norway for instance, caused us a lot of inconvenience only last year. They must never be underestimated. In your case, that means Bruce especially. Like they say in the gangster pictures, that guy is plenty smart copper. Where was I?"

It didn't seem to Laura that he'd really lost the thread. He was probably just ensuring she was paying attention.

"You were about to say what happens when operatives become known."

"Right. Well, they have to drop out. Die if possible."

From the casual way he said it, she guessed he didn't mean it quite literally.

"Die?" she echoed.

"Yup. It can be complicated of course. Particularly if there's a lot of family or business commitments. We arrange something, a boat trip, a foreign holiday. The patient dies. We get him away to another area altogether, different part of the world. There we fix him up a completely new identity and he carries on as normal. If normal is an appropriate word in this context."

"Scarcely," she smiled. "And what is the great decision in my case?"

"How would you feel about dying, Mrs. Kilburn? You have, excuse me, lost your husband. You haven't any real close family ties. Businesswise, you're freelance. Would it come too hard to drown Laura Kilburn at sea?"

What a question. She studied the floor very hard, her mind racing with a hundred problems, conflicting emotions.

"Do I have to decide right now, right this minute?"

He thought about that before replying.

"In the ordinary way, there's no time for shilly-shallying around. But there's no desperate hurry here as I see it. We have a breathing space while you're undergoing training. No, I think we could give you two or three weeks to think about it. Besides, we don't like to have to do these things unless they're essential. In a few weeks we may know more about just how good your personal security is. Let's leave it that way for now."

They were interrupted by a sharp

buzzing in the tiny hall.

"That'll be the doctor," Monahan said, rising.

"Doctor? But surely I can manage with — "

"No," he said decisively. "You can get the cuts to heal, certainly. But if you don't want to be scarred, and it would be a great pity, you need expert attention. Say nothing to this man outside of normal chit-chat. He's not one of us."

He left her, to answer the door. Laura sat quite still, contemplating this new side of Monahan. Not many men would have been thoughtful enough to think of scars, the way a woman would concern herself over them. And concern had already formed in her mind.

The doctor was a brisk, cheerful man in his fifties. He took Laura into the bedroom, and it was obvious he was no stranger to the place. He told her to remove the jacket, and tutted at the amateur way in which the plasters had been applied.

"I'm afraid I'm going to have to hurt you a bit," he said formally.

Laura gritted her teeth as the plasters were removed by deft, expert fingers.

"Oh dear," he muttered, "these are nasty, very nasty."

"What I'm worried about doctor is whether they'll heal so as to leave me scarred for life."

"H'm let's see. No. I think we can assure you on that. An unusually sharp instrument was used here, so there's no tearing of the skin. Yes, I think I can manage this for you. It will entail no great physical exertion on your part for at least five days. Can you promise that? It's not an earthly bit of good my doing a first-class job, if you're going to ruin it."

"I see that, and I'll remember."

He was quick, and professional, asking no questions. When he was finished he stood up.

"Those dressings must not be disturbed. If you take my advice, you'll have them removed by an expert, just in case healing is slow. Goodnight."

He went out, and Laura shrugged her way back into the jacket, leaving the bedroom. There were voices from the hall, then the front door closed. Monahan entered.

"All O.K.?" he asked.

"Very much better," she assured him. "And I want to thank you for thinking about my being disfigured."

"Forget it," he said almost brusquely.

"Tell me, if that doctor isn't one of us," and she realized how she relished the 'us', the confirmation of her acceptance, "why did he take the whole thing in his stride like that? He didn't ask even one question. Can he be trusted?"

"Implicitly. The man's a crook. Spends most of his time patching up slashed prostitutes, and fishing bullets out of West End thugs. Needn't worry about him. And now, let's make use of what's left of the night."

There must have been a question on her face, because the Irishman shook his head, unsmilingly.

"You needn't concern yourself about me, Mrs. Kilburn. You nor any other woman. Not yet. Some day perhaps, but not yet. Johann's sister was my girl. It takes a man a time to recover."

"I'm sorry. I didn't mean to act like a frightened child."

"Perfectly natural. Forget it. You take the bedroom, I'll flop out in here. Tomorrow you can sleep late. We don't have to leave till around eleven."

With her hand on the bedroom door handle, Laura turned. "I haven't anything to wear," she remembered.

"There are a few things in there, if you can find some to fit. No, don't look so worried. They weren't hers."

Five minutes later Laura was in a deep dreamless slumber.

14

At noon the next day they were well clear of London. Laura leaned her head back, lulled by the green hedges speeding by on either side. This morning she felt good, surprised again at how remote the horrors of the previous night had become. She had slept heavily, woken at ten o'clock. Monahan had already brewed excellent coffee, and she busied herself making them some scrambled eggs. He was a relaxing person to be with, chattering aimlessly about non-essentials. They could have been a suburban couple, she reflected at one stage, a reflection which was marred by the unexpected discovery of a dark blue automatic on the dresser. The amiable lout drifting about the place in bare feet seemed a very different person from the gunman of a few hours before. But she had been there, had seen him with that other face. Yet curiously she did not find him repellent because of it. Probably, she decided in her practical fashion, because she had been the beneficiary.

"You know this part of the world?"

It was his first word in ten miles. She broke off her day-dreaming.

"No. No, I don't think I've ever been this way."

"We'll be at the house in twenty minutes. Normally, I'd have to blindfold you about now, but I think you're too far in for it to be necessary."

The words 'too far in' sounded a bit ominous, but he probably hadn't meant them to be. Soon they turned off a side road into a wide sweeping drive, and emerging from a belt of trees, came into view of the house. It was lovely, as she had judged from her previous limited views. The kind of place handed out to favourites of both sexes by medieval monarchs. She wondered fleetingly what tales the place could tell, of intrigues and romances, skirmishes perhaps and treachery. Not that anything in its past was likely to be more bizarre than its present use. The large double front doors had opened as the car came to a halt. Sven came out, smiling, dressed in the now familiar black overalls.

"It is good to see you Mrs. Kilburn," he greeted. "They say you did very well. That is nice."

"Hullo Sven."

She shook his hand as though they were old friends. Her mind went back to her first meeting with the man in the white mask, and she wondered whether she would see him on this visit. Her unspoken question was soon answered.

"The master regrets, Michael, but he will not find it possible to see you on this occasion. He has left full instructions."

"Fine," acknowledged Monahan cheerfully, "I dare say we can amuse ourselves for a few hours."

At the end of which time, what? thought Laura. Sven led them to a large airy room, thickly lined with books.

"I may get you a drink perhaps?" suggested the blond man.

"You may get us a drink, positively," asserted Monahan. "What'll it be, honey?"

255

"Let's see gin and tonic?"

"Good," he agreed. "With the accent on the gin, eh Sven?"

Sven hesitated, then shrugged.

"I do not think it will harm. You are not operational. Very well, I will get them."

As he left the room, Monahan winked at her.

"One thing they keep locked up around here all the time, and that is the old liquor cupboard. There's only one man they trust with the key, and that's Sven."

"Is he Swedish?" she ventured.

"Not really sure. Danish, I think. We don't ask each other too many questions. It isn't that we don't trust each other, but what we literally don't know can't be tortured out of us."

Some of the sunlight seemed to fade from the room as he said it. It sounded casual, but Laura had good reason to know what a serious statement it was. Sven came back then, breaking what could have been an uneasy silence. On a silver tray he carried two tall tumblers. Evidently, he did not intend to join them. Laura tipped her glass towards the American.

"Skol."

"Mud in yours," he returned. "Well, where's the envelope?"

"It is here."

Sven unbuttoned a breast pocket and drew out a small white square, passing it to Monahan. He ripped it open and withdrew a folded single sheet of paper.

"Man of few words, the master," he said slowly. "Still, it tells us all we need to know. And it's what I expected. Beautiful lady, we are going on a little trip."

"I know better than to ask where."

"Good for you. However, this time you can be told. We're going to Africa."

She almost slopped her drink in surprise.

"I'm sure I heard you the first time," she said slowly, "but it was something like Africa wasn't it?"

"Exactly like it," he nodded. "You like?"

"Well, I don't know, I mean, I have to think, I mean —

The two men chuckled looking at

each other. Laura had a good sip at her drink. Africa. She'd always wanted to go, never had the time or the money in the past. Not until John's death. After that she hadn't wanted to do anything very much.

"But my passport," she exclaimed. "The superintendent told me not to leave the country."

"We'd hate to get you in Dutch with the superintendent," said Monahan mock-seriously. "Tell you what, we won't tell him. Next trip for Africa leaves the roof at nine-thirty sharp. Come here a minute."

He walked over to one wall, where a large map hung.

"We'll lift off in the chopper at nine-thirty. Our first job is to rendezvous with Big Momma at — "

"Big Momma?" interjected Laura.

"That's our mother-ship. You homed in on her the other night. Remember?"

Of course. And Big Momma was a very apt name. Laura admitted.

"Yes. Silly question. Please go on."

"Well now, Big Momma can't give

us a precise E.T.A because she doesn't know it herself yet. The crew have to monitor all and every flight route switch on internal and international air lines, right up to almost the last minute. We can't risk any accident, and not even a near accident. Innocent people might get heart seizure, or some other disaster. So they have to keep listening, checking, till they're sure they have some clear air space for eight to ten minutes. Then we close in on the old girl and that's the first leg."

"Sounds good."

Laura tried to sound nonchalant. After all, it was surely a commonplace matter for a girl to be piloting an unlighted helicopter in the night skies? To be making a newsworthy entry to a mother ship in the total darkness? Subsequently to effect illegal departure from her home country, and presumably equally illegal entry to another country?

But it *was* exciting. She began to feel the familiar tingling in her blood. Whether it was the flying, the test of her nerves and skill, the comradeship, the prospect of Africa, she didn't know. Perhaps it was a combination of all these. And in addition the sense of purpose, the feeling of having a job to do, something that was worthwhile, something to lift her away from the deadness of that life she had known without John. Whatever it was, she decided, this is for me. This is for Laura Kilburn.

The two men had remained silent all this while. It could have been born out of the normal male deference to a woman. Or it could have been the intuitive understanding of equals in an unusual situation. Certainly, Monahan sensed the moment when it was opportune to speak again. As though at the end of some questionable males-only joke, he suddenly said:

" — so the bishop said, Madam, that's precisely what happened last time."

He joined Sven in a quick laugh. Laura snapped to herself.

"Sorry, did I miss the joke?"

"Lady, it was not for your tiny pear-shaped ears," Monahan reproved gravely.

"Most unsuitable," said Sven, equally

serious. "In fact I did not approve it myself."

"Approve *of* it, you Nordic heathen. At least you could loin de langwidge of de country which feeds ya."

It was a joke between them. They grinned broadly at one another, while Laura felt like a spectator at some private encounter.

"Are you going to tell me about the second leg?"

"Sure. With luck we will make contact between ten and ten-thirty. Then we have nothing to do all night. They'll probably roust us out at five a.m. or thereabouts. By that time we shall be here, give or take a couple of hundred miles."

Laura had followed the pointing finger as it traced its way down into the heart of the African continent.

"You know what this territory is? Or do you get confused with all these new names, like a lot of people?"

"I'm afraid I do," she confessed.

"Zenafra," he informed her. "Now does it ring a bell?"

"Yes. That was where they had that

261

terrible war a couple of years ago. The United Nations were involved."

She could remember the awful reports and pictures of atrocities. Remember the politicians, not only of the countries concerned, but also of the big East and West blocs, talking, debating, doing nothing.

"Zenafra," stated Monahan, with quiet pride, "was one of our biggest successes."

The astonishment on her face was genuine.

"I'll have to ask you to explain that."

"All right." He went and sat down on the edge of the desk, swinging his legs. "The Zenafran people are not a warrior race. They are farmers, musicians, happy people. They are also very advanced by comparison with some other African nations, and have produced many fine scholars. Those brutes to the north have always hated them, and once the British moved out, they figured they may as well take over. They invaded, thinking they'd take the place over in a couple of weeks. The Zenafrans thought different. They'd expected something of the kind, long before Independence, and they were ready. They played a hit and run war, the way old Shaka had done years before. Striking from cover and melting back into the forest. The invasion forces could never get them involved in a pitched battle. It couldn't last, of course. Zenafra had virtually no guns, only half a dozen ancient aircraft. We knew the big countries would try to keep their hands clean. They'd done it before, in the Congo, Nigeria, other places. Nobody was going to help poor little Zenafra. So the Council decided to act immediately. They sent in every mobile unit in the organization. We took in enough arms and ammunition for the whole army, plus a few fighter planes. At first, they didn't trust us, but knew they had little or no choice. We ran the whole war. Man, it was the weirdest army you ever saw. Every nationality and colour you could put a name to, every man a trained expert at something or other. The West said we were Moscow trained, the East we were capitalist mercenaries. All we asked from Zenafra was complete anonymity, and we got it. We wore green jungle outfits with Australian bush hats. Did you ever see a Chinaman in an Australian bush hat? You'd never forget it. Well, the campaign lasted three months, then the boys from the north hollered uncle. Those Zenafrans could fight like tigers, once somebody had shown them how to do it. When it was over, we offered to build a strongpoint, one mile inside the border, and fly patrol on the border every day. There would be no more surprise attacks. They provided the labour, and what materials they could. We provided the know how, and anything else they were short of."

"And that's where we're going?"

"That's it. It's one of our main bases. Nobody ever comes near the place, nobody asks questions. We use it for training, for stores, all kinds of things. It's practically inaccessible except from the air. If any of the boys next door ever get nosy, we just pump up a few anti-aircraft shells and they go away."

Laura was silent, thinking over Monahan's story. Reflecting too, what a really large-scale organization she was in. Then she had a thought.

"But is there any water large enough for a ship the size of Big Momma to land?"

"Lord, no. We just get in the chopper and fly the last few miles by ourselves."

"Sounds marvellous."

It did, too. She stared again at the map, at the dark green area indicating thick vegetation. It was almost incredible to reflect that she would be there in a matter of hours.

"How will you pass the day, Mrs. Kilburn?" queried Sven. "You could rest if you wish, or walk in the grounds. Whatever you like."

She decided to walk. Monahan did not offer to accompany her, and for this she was glad. With so much on her mind, she preferred to be alone. Later, they had some food, and she spent the early evening sitting in the grounds enjoying the peace.

Monahan came for her at seven and asked her to give the helicopter a thorough inspection. Once again, she found herself up on the now familiar black roof, where the helicopter squatted like an old friend. She went to work very carefully, missing nothing. After an hour, Monahan came up to see what progress she was making.

"Will it fly?" he greeted.

"H'm," she muttered, preoccupied. "You know, Monahan — "

"You could make it Mike," he suggested.

"You know, Mike, I've been thinking about oil, and some of the lubrication, too. I've never done any flying in the tropics but I know one has to pay particular attention to all greases. Is there a book on maintenance in the house?"

He winked at her cheerfully approval large on his face.

"I knew you were going to make good around here. Matter of fact, you can forget it. There's a special crew on Big Momma who will take care of all that for us, while we're asleep."

"Fine. Well, that was my only point. Otherwise she's first rate."

"Then let's go down and have some coffee. It won't be long now."

After coffee, he took her to a room where she could change into her own black overalls. There was a small bag on a table, into which she could pack whatever underclothes, shoes, etc., she selected.

At nine-twenty they both shook hands formally with Sven, who wished them good luck. At nine-thirty precisely, the black chopper lifted off into the night sky.

15

Somebody was tugging at her shoulder. Laura shrugged irritably, then came suddenly awake. A large negro smiled encouragingly.

"Time you were up, Mrs. Kilburn. We part company in twenty minutes."

Twenty minutes. She swung her legs off the narrow bunk, and splashed water quickly on her face from the basin in the corner. The comforting thudding of Big Momma's engines was not quite muffled by the steel door. There was no window in the tiny cabin, so she had no way of telling if it was yet dawn. A quick repair job on her face and hair, and she went out into the corridor. Monahan was leaning against the wall, smoking.

"Want some coffee?"

"No thanks. Too excited. I'll have a cigarette, though. And is there such a thing as a window on this aircraft?"

"Sure, come on."

He opened a hatch door, into a small compartment exactly like that of a regular passenger-carrying machine. There were windows on either side, and strong early light filled the cabin. Laura hopped into the nearest seat, and stared down. There it was. Most countries she had been to were indistinguishable from each other from the air. But this was without question Africa. There were the dense forests, the broad slow rivers, the high brown plateaux. Impatiently, she screwed up her eyes in an attempt to locate wild life, knowing that from this height it would be impossible.

"Oh Mike," she breathed, "isn't that absolutely wonderful?"

"Yup," he admitted. "Most places I can take or leave alone, but Africa does something to you. Something special. I've been a dozen times, lived here, fought here, but I always feel that same pull whenever I come back. Come on, it's almost time you got a real close look."

Reluctantly, she followed him out, and down to the bay where the helicopter rested. The maintenance crew were there, and she chatted with them about the special tropical greases they had applied. Then she climbed up into the pilot's seat, Monahan beside her. Laura switched on the engine, eyes fixed on the Z-box. The red and green lights sprang suddenly to life, and she lifted the Rondo the regulation three feet from the floor of the ship. Then the floor broke into two neat halves, and far below the jungle rushed under them. Steadily, she lowered into the gap, watching the lights. The green one began to flash intermittently, and she took the helicopter three feet further down. There, in front of her was the metal shield. She had sixty more seconds before drop-off. Once again she checked that her door was securely locked, motioning Monahan to do the same. He gave the thumbs up sign, and she tightened her hand on the throttle. There went the light. She pushed the throttle hard home, dipping the Rondo's nose steeply at the same instant. At once the little ship was caught in the violence of the airstream to which they were now exposed. She hung on grimly as they tossed about, nursing the machine back to control.

"Phew," she uttered.

Monahan laughed, patting her shoulder.

"You want to try it some time when there's a gale. That is really something. You see that mountain, the taller of the two directly ahead?"

"Yes."

"Just aim for it. That's the one Zenafrans call Big Bird Hill. There's a tale about some giant bird used to roost on the top. Takes some believing, but it's a nice story. Why don't we go down to a couple of hundred feet? You can enjoy the view."

She did as he suggested, and was soon lost in contemplation of the spectacular spread out below.

"Getting close now. About one mile dead ahead. There, now. See? That's the look-out tower."

A tall pillar of concrete and glass came into perspective, incongruous against the natural surroundings. Laura headed for it, and now could see figures gathered on the roof, watching them approach.

"Go past the tower, keeping it on your right. Then slow right down, and you'll see where we drop."

They passed within twenty feet of the men on the roof, who seemed very interested. Then they were over what was clearly a fort. High white walls formed a huge rectangle, the middle of which was kept free of any obstructions. There was another black Rondo outside the line of buildings which abutted one wall.

"Next to our twin brother there?"

"Right."

They went down smoothly, and Laura switched off.

"This is like Fort Zinderneuf," she remarked, climbing out.

"Huh?"

Monahan looked puzzled.

"Beau Geste," she explained. "You know, the French Foreign Legion."

"Oh, sure. Well, I think you'll find we're a little more comfortable than those guys. Come on and meet some people."

Little knots of men had appeared at various doorways. Monahan waved to some calling them by name. Then he led her into one of the larger buildings. As the doors closed easily behind them, Laura noted the sharp drop in temperature. At a table in the corner, a man in an immaculate white suit put down a coffee cup and rose to his feet. He was very tall, probably six feet seven or eight inches, and had a bronzed face, which would have been handsome but for the perpetual wryness of his mouth. He looked as though everything had happened to him already, and he expected momentarily that it was all going to happen again. He spoke in English, but it was clearly not his mother tongue.

"Mrs. Kilburn, a great pleasure. Monahan, how are you?"

"Fine thanks, Sherba, no trouble on the trip. Laura this is Sherba. He is the boss man around here. You and I can get on with what we came for, but for all other matters, we do as he says."

"How do you do?"

Laura shook hands with her new boss, who smiled his encouragement.

"As you see, I am just finishing breakfast. We rise early here. Please sit and join me. We shall have coffee, we shall talk. Then I must leave you, and you can have a proper breakfast."

They sat down. Sherba had coffee cups ready, and poured from a shining metal percolator. Laura wrinkled her nose appreciatively.

"It is one of the minor blessings of our little community. Some of the finest coffee in the world is grown only one hundred miles from here. Now, how much does the lady know?"

"Nothing. I didn't have clearance. Anyway, I don't know too much myself," Monahan reported.

"Very well. Mrs. Kilburn, it is routine here for newcomers to undergo a rigorous period of training. It lasts only ten days, and I am sure in your case, it is largely unnecessary. The report is that you are in splendid physical condition. Yes?"

Laura wanted to interrupt him.

"Look, I hate to make a fuss, but I have some scars. The doctor said I ought not to exert myself too much for — "

"I know, and it is allowed for. The physical side of the training has been put

274

to the end of the period. Initially you will concentrate on weapon training."

"Thank you." These people thought of everything.

"This is not a vacation resort," he went on. "Your presence here is costing money, and we must ensure that your time is usefully employed. We rise at six, breakfast at six-thirty. We work from seven till eleven, then break for one hour. Lunch is at twelve. In the afternoons, some have assignments, and some not. You will be one of those who works. There is a break at four, which was insisted on by certain of our people from England. At this curious hour there is tea. The break is twenty minutes. Work continues until six. After that our time is our own, except for those on duty. We dine at eight, and there is usually a film at nine-thirty for those interested. I hope you have brought some in?" he asked Monahan.

"Yes, some good ones. There's a Cary Grant, couple of Westerns, and two or three continental films. Something for everyone, I think."

"Good. Well, that is our programme, Mrs. Kilburn. It is not exciting but I think your stay here will not be long enough for you to become bored. Now there remains the question of your quarters. We are not accustomed to women. I have had a room in this building prepared for you. This is the administration block by the way. There is a bathroom here, and I think you will find everything you need. However, do not hesitate to ask, if our male preparations have overlooked anything."

"Thank you, I am sure I shall manage."

"And one more thing." Sherba stared at her steadily. "We shall do all we can to treat you as an equal. However, the fact remains that you are a woman, and extremely attractive. There are men here from all walks of life, all levels of society. All hand picked for one skill or another, all self-reliant, courageous people. A bit tough, if you like. They have their instructions, but they are men. I think I make my point?"

"I'll be careful," she nodded. "And I'll try to avoid provoking them."

"Good. I hope you will enjoy your stay. And now I must go. I may see you at lunch."

He rose, bowed and went out.

"Did somebody mention breakfast?" Monahan got up, stretching. "I could eat a horse. How about you?"

"Well, I'm not too keen on horse, but almost anything else. What do we do, shout?"

He shook his head.

"No, we don't eat here. This is Sherba's private dining-room. We have to go over to the commissary. You want to see your room first?"

"Yes, please."

"It's through here."

They went into the next room which was kitted out with office equipment. Beyond that was the radio room, an impressive set, larger than many Laura had seen on small airfields. The room lay beyond, and Laura was impressed. It was not a question of a makeshift bed, as she'd half expected. The place was extremely comfortable, with curtains and carpeted floor. There was a comfortable chair and a deep settee. The bathroom adjoined.

"Why this is a private suite," she exclaimed admiringly. "They've done wonders."

Beside her, Monahan chuckled.

"They haven't done a darned thing," he contradicted. "Sherba moved out, that's all."

"You mean he gave this up for me? I must go and thank him."

"Not now, honey. He won't have his schedule interrupted. You'll get your chance later. Right now, the thing is breakfast."

They went back the way they'd come, and out into the now brilliant sunlight. The heat struck Laura almost like a blow, glaring back from the white walls of the compound.

"Rule one," announced Monahan. "Don't roam around here in the daytime without sunglasses. You'll get a headache within one hour, and you won't shake it too fast. The commissary is that big building there."

They hugged the shade of the sloping

wooden roof that extended a few feet from the side of each building, making a kind of shelter. The commissary was a long rectangular room, with kitchens at the far end. Tables were set out in long neat rows. There was no one eating.

"Think we're too late?" queried Laura.

"Good Lord no. How could a beauty like yourself be late, me girl? 'Tis all the others was early."

A booming Irish voice answered her question, and she saw the owner, a large beaming man, appear behind the counter at the far end.

"Hi, Ryan. How've you been?"

Monahan grinned at the Irishman.

"Sure and I've no time to waste on you, while I've this lovely lady here to look at. Ryan, ma'am, Sean Ryan at your service. And if I say so meself, the finest cook in the tropics."

Laura smiled. The man's humour was infectious.

"Hallo Sean Ryan. I'm Laura Kilburn, and I'm all set to be greatly impressed with your skill at eggs and bacon, toast and coffee. If available."

"Unworthy of me talents, but for you, anything."

He disappeared from sight, and within minutes was back with a heaped tray. This he handed to Laura, along with a liberal helping of extravagant compliments. She and Monahan lost no time in attacking the food, and soon they were sitting back, dawdling over an extra cup of coffee.

"It hardly seems possible."

They were Laura's first words for several minutes, and startled the American out of his reverie.

"Huh? What does?"

"That I'm really here. I'll say one thing for this organization. Life can hardly be said to be dull."

"It's the nature of the structure," he explained. "Our purpose for existence is to get things done. We don't have to concern ourselves with paperwork, or a lot of administration. Not us," he amended. "The field operators, that is. There are people who do all that for us. We're the glory brigade really, always on the move, always where the action is.

That is our speciality, our *raison d'être*, if you like."

She listened seriously, paying full attention to his words.

"What's it like really, Mike? I mean, I ought to know now, since it looks as though I'm in over my ears."

He tapped ash into the square glass tray.

"It isn't always comfortable," he admitted. "But you've already seen a little of that side yourself. As to the rest, I guess each man holds his own views. You'll come to yours in time. Now let's go and look the place over."

The palaver is ended, thought Laura. They spent the next couple of hours wandering around, meeting people, and getting her acquainted with the layout of the place. She learned, among other things, that her training schedule would not begin till the following day.

"So we have free time," she pointed out. "Are there any excursions?"

"All the time," she was assured gravely. "Coaches depart from the main gate every hour on the hour."

It was arranged that Monahan would take her sightseeing in one of the jeeps, which was promised for after lunch, a splendid meal which Laura suspected was rather grander than usual, in her honour. Afterwards, she sat entranced, as the jeep bounced over the rutted jungle tracks, watching the wildlife, and absorbing the impact of the riotous vegetation.

"Make the most of this little ride," advised Mike. "Next time you come this way you'll be carrying a pack, rifle and ammunition. Twenty miles the first day, and it steps up from there."

"Sounds like fun," she said ruefully.

"It isn't. It isn't intended to be. I'm not looking forward to it either."

"You too? But you've done it all before," she exclaimed.

"Sure. They like to be positive I can still do it. Matter of fact," he added confidentially, "it makes you feel pretty good when you have done it. Kid's stuff really, but you can't help a sense of achievement."

Probably an achievement I could live

282

without, but she kept her thoughts to
herself.

* * *

Immediately after breakfast the next
morning she was handed over to a
tall silent man who was called simply
Haroun. His dark skin, and hawk-like
features proclaimed him to be an Arab,
and the piercing eyes suggested perhaps
one of the great nomadic tribes. Not that
Laura had much time for idle speculation
of that kind.

"Mrs. Kilburn, what is your knowledge
of hand weapons?"

She told him about her brief encounter
with the .38.

"And that is all? No machine guns, no
rifles, no automatic rifles, no revolvers?"

"None, I'm afraid."

Disapproval was not far from the
surface of his tone.

"Then I regret, we have much work to
do. Please come with me."

He led her past rack after rack of
gleaming weapons, finally pulled one

from its retaining clips and laid it on a table.

"There are many types of weapon here. It is necessary that you know something of each of them. You cannot learn all intimately, as you should. We will concentrate on a few. There are certain principles which are common to many, and these again you must know. The weapon before you was general issue to a large proportion of the United States forces in the recent war with Germany and Japan. It is .30 calibre, a rifle, and is known as the M.1."

He handled the gun expertly, almost fondly, as he went through the motions of stripping and cleaning. Laura had never had any cause to wonder about such things, wonder what made them into the deadly efficient lethal weapons they were. Hitherto she had only known that you pointed them at someone, pulled a trigger, and the someone was shot. How or why it happened had never concerned her. The taciturn Haroun was filling in this gap in her knowledge.

"A rifle, or any weapon, is a precision

machined tool. Nothing more, nothing less. It is not of itself evil, neither does it threaten. It becomes merely the instrument of evil in the hands of evil men. You must know this and understand it. Such a weapon is to be trusted. It will never let you down. It has been made, and made by experts, to perform certain functions at your command. As I say, it will never let you down. But unless you know your weapon, recognize it as the tool it is, you can let yourself down. Like most Western women, you are no doubt the owner of a motor car?"

It seemed an odd question, but Laura nodded.

"Yes, I have a car. What's the connection?"

"This car now, you take it to experts from time to time. They do things to it, things perhaps you do not understand?"

"Why, of course."

"And frequently, you put things into this car. Gasoline, oil, water?"

She was getting the idea now and merely nodded.

"As you say, of course. If you did not,

the car would not proceed. And if that should happen, you would not say, this damn car she has let me down. No. You would say, it is my fault, I forgot to fill the tank. I think you have my meaning, Mrs. Kilburn. A weapon is no different. There are things you must do. There are things also, you must not do. You must never point it at someone, unless you are prepared to pull the trigger. You must never leave ammunition inside unless you expect to have to use it. You must never rest it on the ground, barrel down. You must never let it get wet, if this can possibly be avoided. Those are some of the things you must not do. There are others, we will speak of those later. And now, I will ask you to dismantle this rifle, as you have watched me do."

She grasped it, gingerly at first, and made her first fumbling movements. Haroun was a good instructor, patient with her. By the time he released her for a welcome lunch, she was reasonably proficient with the U.S. M.I., the Spandau machine pistol, the British

Lee Enfield rifle, and the Thompson submachine gun.

There was so much to do and learn, that the day and the days that followed went swiftly by. Once, remembering Sherba's injunction about sex problems, Laura chuckled wryly to herself. She was too bone-weary to notice, even if somebody did try to make a pass at her. Before and after dinner each night, she found herself poring busily over the maintenance instruction manuals for the next batch of weapons. Haroun would cross-examine her mercilessly at the next session, as she had learned early in the course.

Then at lunch one day, there was a message that Sherba wished to see her in his office. She tapped at his door, and went in.

"Ah Mrs. Kilburn, please sit down."

It was an airy, pleasant room, with certain austere comforts. She lowered herself into an upright armchair. He smiled, and moved a cigarette box before her.

"No thank you, I just put one out."

"Very well. Mrs. Kilburn I have Haroun's report on your progress."

Oh God, she thought. It's because of the jamming on that Sten gun. Pity, that. Up till then she'd fancied she wasn't doing too badly. Sherba tapped at the paper with strong fingers.

"In the weapon training establishments of the armed forces of your country, ten days are allowed for the achievement of a certain standard. This is a generous time, and is intended to cover a wide range of people. Since our people are in the higher intelligence brackets, we expect that standard to be reached in five days."

Five days. Well, he wasn't giving her a proper chance, she thought resentfully. She'd only been at it three and a half days.

"Haroun is a most capable and competent instructor. He is always scrupulously fair to trainees, and none of his reports has ever been questioned. His report on you Mrs. Kilburn — "

Here it comes, she thought.

" — states that he is satisfied after

three and a half days with you, that the standard has been achieved. It is a most remarkable effort on your part. Quite the best performance we have had. I should like to offer my most sincere congratulations."

Confused, Laura rose to take the outstretched hand. A record, he'd said. Well, what do you know. And she'd thought that old devil Haroun didn't like her.

"I — I don't know what to say. I really don't."

"Then say nothing, dear lady. Please sit and compose yourself."

"Could I change my mind about that cigarette?"

He lit it for her, and she was chagrined to see her hand trembling slightly.

"I would like to proceed to the next phase as quickly as possible. The doctor will examine your scars at four o'clock, to see what healing progress has been made. Not that you will be called upon for any violent exertions for three more days. In the meantime, no doubt you have been warned about the marches?"

"Yes. By two or three people," she acknowledged.

"You will start tomorrow. I considered making some concessions as to our requirements because you are a woman. However, having had the pleasure of talking to you and observing you these past days, I have come to the view that it is not necessary. Also, unless I am mistaken, you would not wish it?"

"No," she said decisively. "I don't want to get in on a free ticket, or as a second class citizen. I'll do the same as the others."

"Exactly so. Very well, you start in the morning."

The doctor was a red-bearded Russian who clucked approvingly at the progress of her wounds.

"Experts here," he barked. "These incisions were made by an expert, and the repair work was done also by an expert. Perhaps I know him?"

"I hope not. He's a doctor who works exclusively on London criminals," she said slyly.

The Russian harrumphed a few times,

and told her to see him again in two days. She spent the rest of that day in splendid idleness, and was up earlier than usual next morning. As she said to Monahan at breakfast, she had misgivings about the thick socks and the heavy lace-up boots she'd been given.

"You'll be glad of 'em, honey. Tonight, your feet will be weary. But if you didn't have the proper equipment, they'd be in ribbons."

They started off the march in almost holiday spirit, but after the first three miles there was little banter left in them. After five miles there was no conversation at all. The rough, broken terrain demanded every bit of their physical resources. Laura had quickly found her own version of the heavy-footed infantry trudge which was the only way to walk under such conditions. Apart from herself and Monahan, there were three other men in the little force, the leader and two others. She'd seen them in the distance before, and had thought the expedition would provide an opportunity of getting to know some different people.

But, after a few miles, she was oblivious to those around her. The world had become a very small place, where the only serious considerations were what relief could be brought to certain muscles by a displacement of the rifle and pack, and how long the new muscles thus brought into play could sustain the burden. Then too, there was the vital matter of putting this foot in front of the other, and a careful study of the ground immediately ahead, so that any avoidable stone or ridge of hard packed earth could be spotted in time. Larger matters, such as direction, distance and the passage of time, were not for her. It needed all she had to keep plodding forward. The announcement of a thirty minute rest for lunch came as a shock. She had privately assessed that a twenty mile hike should take five hours. Add a little for contingencies such as weight carried and the thing should be completed comfortably in six hours.

After lunching on the pack rations each of them carried, washed down by the tepid water in their bottles, they pushed on again. Finally, the look-out tower came into view. As they staggered wordlessly through the gates, Sherba was watching them.

"Not bad," he told the leader. "Eleven hours. Well up to standard."

Laura heard the words faintly, not believing them. Eleven hours.

"We made it, honey."

The croaking voice, hardly recognizable as Monahan's sounded close by.

"What does he mean, eleven hours?" she queried. "It can't be. Why, we've only done twenty miles."

"It can be, and it is. You can't apply ordinary measures. We didn't do so bad."

Lying in the bath afterwards, Laura decided that heaven must be a place liberally supplied with bathrooms, and endless hot water. She was too bone-weary to turn out for dinner, and instead went straight to bed.

Hours later, there was an insistent loud knocking at her door. Looking at her watch, she realized she hadn't switched off the light. And look at the time. Three a.m.

293

"What is it?" she called irritably.

"Mrs. Kilburn, there is an emergency," replied a loud voice. "Please get dressed immediately and report to Sherba's office. There is someone to see you."

Emergency. Well, there wasn't any point in arguing.

"All right, I'll come at once."

What emergency, and who could there possibly be to see her in this outlandish place?

Reluctantly she pushed back the covers.

16

The jungle night air struck cold in the room as she hurried around, getting ready. A final quick inspection in the mirror, and she decided she would do. Or, more accurately, would have to do. Soon she was knocking at Sherba's door.

Walking in, she almost stopped in surprise. Seated behind the desk was not Sherba, but the man in the white mask.

"Good evening, Mrs. Kilburn. It is a pleasure to see you again. Please come and sit down."

The melodious, slightly foreign voice, took her back to that first night when all this had started.

"Good evening," she returned.

Recovering from the initial shock, she now saw Nagumi seated at the end of the room, with Sherba. The Japanese gave her a reassuring nod, and she smiled as at an old friend.

"Mrs. Kilburn, I know you had a strenuous day yesterday, and I regret the necessity for disturbing your rest. Something has come up rather unexpectedly, and you are needed for a cruise."

All tiredness gone, she leaned forward.

"But I haven't finished — " she began.

"There will not be time. This other matter, it is of urgent importance. Our people in Cairo have learned the whereabouts of someone we have been looking for for months. And in circumstances which make the whole cruise of double importance. First, the man. Have you heard of Francesco Pasquale, more often referred to as Frankie Packer?"

"The gangster? The American who was deported a few years ago?"

"That is the man. An evil, corrupt man, responsible for a large proportion of the drug traffic into the United States, directly or indirectly involved in who can guess how many murders. He has been living outside Naples since the United States Government deported him.

Ostensibly he is a retired man, but in fact he has merely transferred his headquarters from one country to another. We have had some little success in interfering with his operations on occasions. Indeed, it was a Pasquale deal that your late husband and Monahan were able to foil."

He paused to let the words sink in. Laura was numbed for a moment. Then she said quietly,

"So this man sent those others to — to kill John."

"We were not certain for a long time about that. We are now."

Again he paused. There was much to tell her, and the masked man wanted to be satisfied that she was listening properly, and not concentrating on this one fact. Finally he continued.

"The man Pasquale has gone to ground for some time past, and we have not been able to locate him. I think I will not need to explain why we wanted to find him?"

"No. I understand."

Again, Laura felt an anticipatory gloating inside. It was similar to the feeling she'd experienced initially, when the masked man had been explaining how her husband's murderers had been repaid. But this time there was an added sensation, because they were talking about something which had not yet happened, something in which she might be able to take part personally. The prospect filled her with savage joy. A momentary doubt prompted her to ask.

"There is no room for any question about this, I imagine? Your information is unimpeachable, so far as Pasquale's involvement in John's murder is concerned?"

"No question whatsoever," was the reply. "These matters are not treated lightly, Mrs. Kilburn. Our investigations are every bit as thorough as those of the great police departments of the world. And, in addition, we frequently have access to sources which they cannot reach."

"Thank you. I won't interrupt again."

"Very well. Nagumi, you obtained much of our other information yourself. Please tell us about it."

Nagumi rose, and came forward to the table. He wasn't addressing Laura directly, and she gathered as he went along, that at least some of his facts were new to the others as well.

"The Middle East oil kingdoms are in the news enough for all of you to be familiar with the story. Small states, with all-powerful rulers, finding themselves overnight with an income of a quarter of a million a day, and so on. One reads stories every week of prodigious welfare undertakings, school systems, hospitals, etc. There are stories also of the private spending of the sheikhs, some not so creditable. It is a fact that the Arab is a gambler, and of this one reads little. The reason is not hard to find. Even at the largest casinos in the south of France and elsewhere, there are very few people who can afford to play with these men, for whom the money itself has little meaning. Besides, they have learned to be circumspect. At one time, a sheikh would occasionally visit Monte Carlo or one of the other large resorts. The fact would be widely reported in the world press.

Many of the cheaper newspapers would take the opportunity to print alongside the story a few old prints of beggars and starving children in the sheikh's home state. Mostly irrelevant and unjustified, but effective nevertheless. The sheikhs were hurt and bewildered by such attacks, and gradually withdrew from publicity of this kind. The situation was ready made for a man with Frankie Packer's curious talents."

The Japanese paused, and helped himself to a glass of water, for all the world like a lecturer at a university.

"Last year, the liner *Matruh* was purchased by a company with a Central American registration. Such matters are always of interest to us, since transactions of this kind frequently mean that the future use of such ships is something which will concern us sooner or later. On this occasion it seemed we were wrong. The Matruh was put on to a combined passenger and cargo carrying service between Durban, South Africa, and Madeira in the Canary Islands. The route chosen was via the Suez Canal and Alexandria. The ship was taken out of service a month ago for what was described as a minor refit. This refitting, we now learn, took the form of converting her to a high class floating casino. She has now left port for sea trials, a routine procedure after refitting. There are no passengers. However, Pasquale or Packer is certainly aboard. Many of the regular crew have been replaced by known waterfront toughs. And at least eight of Packer's top criminal associates are missing from their usual haunts in Naples."

Nagumi now unrolled a map which had been resting on the table.

"According to what we have been able to gather so far, and our visual sightings confirm to date, the Matruh sailed direct to the Persian Gulf. Here, she turned, retraced her route and journeyed along Southern Arabia into the Red Sea, where she is now heading for the Suez Canal. By this route, she has been within easy reach of every oil kingdom of any importance at all. We believe the object is to run a special gambling vacation for as many of the sheikhs as care to join. This way they will be free of publicity, and they will be playing with others in their own income bracket. It was an enormous conception, and seems to be working very well."

It was Sherba who spoke next.

"But these men are rulers. They cannot simply disappear for weeks at a time whenever they choose."

"Ah, but they can," corrected the man in the white mask. "The Premier of France, the President of the United States, no. They could not do these things. But these men rule not by consent, but absolutely. Already five of them have announced imminent hunting trips, visits to the inner regions of their states, a fortnight's meditation, all kinds of things, which virtually mean their whereabouts cannot be checked. And remember also no one in these territories is encouraged to ask. No, we have every cause to believe that our information is correct. Somewhere there," and he jabbed a finger at the Gulf of Suez, "is the Matruh. She carries a small army of the most vicious criminals in the world, and an unknown number of the world's richest men."

"And what is it we are after, apart from Mr. Pasquale?" queried Laura.

"Money, dear lady," was the reply. "How much, it is impossible to say. Perhaps one million, perhaps ten. But all in negotiable currency all untraceable. We need money to operate, and we have many sources. But this is such a golden opportunity, to take large sums from people who can well afford it. So well indeed, that they are even now using this money as gambling chips. A completely legitimate target."

Laura had private reservations about this, but she quelled them.

"This Pasquale and his men, they are almost certainly armed," she objected.

"To the teeth," affirmed Nagumi. "And there is no way we can make a frontal assault without serious loss of life. We can only operate on the Matruh herself. And that is why you are here."

"Thank you Nagumi, I will take over now. Mrs. Kilburn, we have a scheme, one with a good chance of success. To effect it, we must have our own agent on that ship. Every avenue has been explored, and it is an impossible task for a man. The Matruh does not touch any ports. She lies off shore, and her distinguished passengers go out to her either in fast motor launches, or by helicopter. But there is a way for you. It might be unpleasant, I should warn you, but if our timings are right, it is possible you might avoid embarrassment."

She didn't like the sound of that at all but nodded to show she understood.

"You have heard of the Bey of Damasha? Not one of the greatest sheikhs, but a man with an income of almost a million dollars a week. Enough to qualify him for the Matruh. Like many of his kind, the Bey has a great weakness for Western women. He prefers English or American if possible. They must be people of charm and poise, able to appear with him without causing him embarrassment. When the Matruh reaches Alexandria, he has ordered his personal envoy to supply such a woman. This he has done, and the lady is waiting at the Hotel Casablanca in Alexandria itself. Tomorrow, regrettably, she will be taken suddenly ill. The Bey is not a man who regards incompetence lightly. His personal envoy will be only too delighted that such a substitute as yourself is available. You do not seem pleased at the prospect."

"Hardly," she retorted. "I'm willing to do most things for you, but I must say that is a bit — "

"Please. Perhaps when you have heard the plan. Nagumi."

Nagumi nodded, and began to speak in low, urgent tones.

17

Laura chuckled. Lightly at first, then gathering momentum until a raucous, and decidedly unladylike laugh filled the room. Although quite alone, she coughed once, twice, to cover the slip. But really, she could not blame herself. Everything was so preposterous, so unlikely. In her dreams of fantasy, many unlikely images had projected themselves, but none more unlikely than this, which was real.

Here she lay, on a bed made of Heaven alone knew what unlikely gossamer materials. Within reach, certainly, the standard ivory telephone. But, and this was what added the gloss, the touch of unreality, there was also a second receiver, coloured deep plum. Why should she require two telephones, no one had explained, and she was most certainly not going to ask. A femme fatale, and that was her current role, took such things in her stride. As she did the bucket of iced champagne, at ten-forty-five in the morning. Not to mention the silver dish covered with the most appetizing tit-bits which lay to hand. Laura was a practical girl, or so she always thought of herself. The telephones, the champagne, the canapes, these she could encompass. Just. But the clincher, the human being who made it all so unlikely so unreal, had been Mr. Ulfrim. Mr. Ulfrim had just left in some disorder. Not at all the way he had started out.

"Madame Kilburn?"

"Ah yes. You must be Mr. — er Mr. — please forgive me, I am terribly bad at names."

"Ulfrim. That is U-L-F-R-I — "

"Yes, of course. How are you, Mr. Ulfrim? Some champagne, perhaps?"

"Madame, you are very kind. But thank you, no. You see — "

"I quite understand. You are a busy man. Please sit down."

He did so. Laura studied him covertly. Without doubt, a very unpleasant little man, and one to be watched. The expressionless almond eyes had seen many things. Things she preferred not to think about. But the important thing to remember was, that Ulfrim was her ticket aboard the good ship Matruh. She could not afford to allow her automatic and natural repugnance to cloud the main issue.

"Well Mr. Ulfrim, I understand you represent certain interests?"

He studied her before replying. Not in any calm, detached way, but with the same kind of involvement a woman would bring to bear in a fish-market before making her choice.

"My master is a most selective, and shall we say, determined man."

"We can say whatever you choose Mr. Ulfrim. Although, candidly, I do not see that it progresses us very far. And, incidentally, I am not much interested in you Mr. Ulfrim, and if you would be good enough to state your business, I shall be obliged. Then, perhaps, I may be allowed to proceed with the important matter of my own existence."

The stress on the word 'important' was intended to leave Mr. Ulfrim in little doubt that his business did not come into that category. He smiled, wryly, not at all perturbed.

"Madame, you are very direct. However, forgive me, I believe you exaggerate. I believe you are interested in my business, otherwise I should not be here. And my business is very much connected at present with the admittedly important one of your existence."

He inclined his head slightly. Laura waved a hand impatiently. It was bad enough to be up for sale, without having to haggle with the middle men.

"Your master, such a handsome and powerful man, has I believe expressed an interest in me. Where was it he saw me? Paris, Rome, New York?"

"I am but a poor messenger. His Eminence does not confide to me the working of his mind. Or his heart. All I am told, is that he is most anxious to meet you, and for you to join his party on the ship. Be assured madame, many leading names of our world will be present. Exalted company, food of the very finest, a few days cruise on the

Mediterranean ocean. What more could one ask?"

He laughed inwardly as he said the last words. She would ask, he had no doubt of it. They sickened him, these perfumed, arrogant women of the west, who could be purchased just as any bazaar harlot. Indeed they were worse, since they made such a pretence. There you see, she was asking.

"What more could one ask?" she laughed briefly. "There is nothing wrong with the food here, Mr. Ulfrim. And I like the company."

"My master is a most generous man. Only last year, one of his lady guests was presented with a silver ashtray."

"A silver ashtray?" she echoed. "I think you are wasting my time. Perhaps you will leave now."

He did not move from his seat.

"Oh, and I almost forgot. This ashtray was filled with precious stones."

Laura lit a cigarette to cover her amusement. This little devil was playing with her.

"Of course, I am very fond of the sea,"

she said musingly.

This time Ulfrim almost let his smile be seen. Almost, but not quite. He was a fortunate man and he knew it. To find any kind of replacement for that other stupid woman had seemed a lost cause. To find such a one as this was little less than a gift from the gods. The Bey was a man who tolerated no incompetence. And when such incompetence was directly associated with his personal pleasure, his wrath was an awesome sight. No, this insolent, arrogant female was more than he had dared to hope for. Indeed she was even more to the precise specifications laid down by his master than his original selection. There remained only the matter of his commission.

"Madame perhaps you could help me."

Laura could not remember the last occasion on which she had dealt with anyone less in need of help.

"If it amuses me," she remarked off-handedly.

"You are very kind. The problem is, there are so many people who wish to accompany my master. So many people, so few invitations. It is difficult for one so modest as myself, to be selective."

She studied the little man. Took in the immaculate linen suit, the silk shirt and tie, the shoes evidently hand-made by Hobbs of London. And he was shouting for his ten per cent. Despite her careful instructions that she must not upset the oily Ulfrim, Laura found herself saying,

"Then of course I can help you."

Ulfrim brightened. Notwithstanding everything else, this was a woman who understood the true values. Inwardly Laura licked her lips.

"The solution is simple. You must discount me."

"Madame?"

The little man's mouth went slack.

"You must leave me off your list. That will make things much easier for you. There, I have helped you, as you asked. And now, I am very tired. I really think it is time you went."

Sickly Ulfrim rose to his feet.

"Madame, perhaps I could re-examine the list. I am sure there will be others who have not your claim to be included in my master's party."

"Nonsense," rejoined Laura, smiling. "You mustn't give it another thought. I am glad to have been able to help you resolve the problem. I know what guest lists are like, Heaven knows."

She felt gay, quite exuberant, as she piloted the obnoxious little man towards the door. Ulfrim's mind was in a whirl. Five minutes ago, the world was an enchanting, profitable place. Now, it lay in ruins around him. It took every ounce of his resources to round on her at the door a wide grin on his face.

"What can I say? Such consideration. I will go at once, and study the lists. If it should be, madame, that you could attend without embarrassment to others perhaps I could telephone you?"

Thank God, thought Laura. For a moment she feared she had overplayed her hand. Now, she could see the olive branch.

"Perhaps," she nodded carelessly. "But it would have to be before three o'clock this afternoon. I had half promised myself that if nothing happened in this boring town by then, I should catch the five o'clock 'plane to Rome."

She felt confident about the time. She knew that the launch bound for the Matruh would not leave harbour until four-thirty. Ulfrim was nodding rapidly.

"By three o'clock. I will remember."

And now he was gone. And here was she, Laura Kilburn, the renowned international adventuress. Plaything of the tycoons, relaxing on her silken spread. Another horse-laugh disturbed the discreet perfumed air.

"La Kilburn," announced Laura gravely, to a non-existent audience, "partook of another stuffed olive. Then quaffing the last of her Veuve Clicquot," which she promptly did, "she composed herself for a couple of hours well-deserved kip."

And she rolled luxuriously on the bed. Within minutes, she was asleep.

She was at lunch in the superb dining-room when the telephone call from Ulfrim came. The head waiter was extremely sorry to disturb her, but —

"There is no 'but'," she reproved him. "I am not to be disturbed during lunch.

Tell whoever it is to call again at two thirty-five precisely."

"Two-thirty-five, madame?" repeated the puzzled majordomo.

"Precisely," she repeated. "I shall finish lunch at two-thirty. I shall be going for a drive at two-forty. The call must be at two-thirty-five."

And it was. The chagrined Ulfrim, who had spent the last several hours in impassioned curses and threats against this ghastly woman, had surrendered. Finally and utterly. Yes, he would bring a car for her at four o'clock. Yes, there would be someone to carry the luggage. Certainly, a personal maid would be available aboard the Matruh. He, Ulfrim, would attend to all this personally. Cradling the receiver, Laura permitted herself a small feeling of self-satisfaction. Revenge Incorporated was undoubtedly a huge and powerful concern, but no amount of planning and organization could supplant a woman's touch.

At four-twenty, she sat beside the now-obsequious Ulfrim, staring with disapproval at a powerful, thirty-foot launch.

"I don't feel at all safe," she said, for the second time. "Just look at those men."

"Madame, I assure you, you were never safer. Certainly these men are lacking in polish. They are hand-picked for their reliability. Their task is to protect the ship's guests. Please madame."

She boarded the launch with some misgivings refusing the hand of one swarthy ruffian who offered to help. The Matruh was out of sight of land, and it was a forty minute trip at speed to reach her. On deck a small group of the ship's officers had gathered, as much from curiosity as hospitality. Ulfrim made no attempt to introduce her.

"You will wish to see your cabin at once, madame. Please come."

There was no sign of the other passengers as he led her inboard. The cabin was spacious, the appointments rich. Laura could see that no expense was being spared.

"Charming," she admitted. "Really quite pleasant. I should like to unpack now, Mr. Ulfrim. When shall I be meeting the other guests?"

"His Eminence will be most pleased to receive you at seven o'clock if this is quite convenient. An aperitif perhaps, in his stateroom?"

"That will be very nice."

He bowed.

"Till seven then."

After he had gone, Laura began to unpack her bags. Looking round at the luxury to which she could very easily become accustomed, she wondered wistfully why the kind of woman she was supposed to be could have such things, while the kind of woman she was seldom got within miles of them. As she slipped into tailored slacks and a nylon blouse, she heard the distant throbbing which announced they were under way.

Unpacking completed, she had only one problem. Where to hide the small .25 automatic Nagumi had supplied, and also a certain parcel. A study of the place quickly showed there was nowhere to hide anything where it could not quickly be found. Her only hope was that no one should have any reason to think it necessary to search. Of course, she remembered, the maid. She would have to be an absolute paragon if she didn't examine everything belonging to her new mistress at the first opportunity. The bathroom cabinet did not lock. Then she had an idea. Lifting the lid of the cistern, she taped both gun and parcel firmly to the underside, then replaced the lid. It would be an unusual maid who would think it profitable to look in such a place. She stood back to admire her handiwork, when there was a tapping at the outer door.

"Come in," she called.

A diminutive dark-haired girl entered, smiling brightly.

"Please madame, I am Louise."

The accent was certainly French.

"Ah yes, you must be the maid."

"Oui, madame. Please, what may I do?"

"Nothing for now, thank you. I have already unpacked. Come back at six-fifteen to help me dress, will you?"

"It shall be so."

She bobbed out again. It was five-twenty, and Laura had the greater part of an hour to herself. Time she could put to good use. She made her way out on deck where a light breeze had sprung up. There were a few people about now, leaning on the rails or strolling decorously along. One or two nodded to her in a friendly way, and she replied with half-smiles. She was not interested in passengers at the moment. There was the man for her. A young deck officer, not much over twenty-one, and resplendent in white linen with gold and black epaulettes.

"Good evening," she smiled warmly.

He saluted gravely. This must be the one who came aboard this afternoon, and a most delectable piece of cargo.

"Good evening, madam. Have you just joined us?"

"Oh yes," she confirmed. "I've a great weakness for ships. I was wondering — that is if you have the time — "

"I am not on duty at the moment, madam. I am at your service."

Laura had to strike a balance between

enlisting his aid, and at the same time avoiding an impression that he was in for a very much more enjoyable time.

"I'd love to see over her. You know, everything. That is, if possible."

Possible. It was most certainly possible. It was also very much to his inclination. Most of them only asked the way to the nearest bar, and what time would the gaming start.

"I shall be very pleased, Miss — ?"

"Mrs. Mrs. Kilburn." Then seeing the shadow on his face, "I'm a widow."

"I am sorry to hear it. Fourth Officer Bernard Slater. Where would you like to begin?"

"I leave it entirely to you, Mr. Slater. I want to see everything."

"Well, this is A deck," he began.

They strolled slowly, Laura asking questions by the dozen. At the stern she asked:

"What are those, are we going to have a firework display?"

Slater laughed. This girl was so bright with some questions, and unaccountably dense with others.

"No, Mrs. Kilburn, those are our signal rockets. For use if we ever get into an emergency."

"Really? Show me how they work."

He showed her the firing mechanism, explaining what had to be done.

"But surely that's dangerous? Supposing one was fired by accident?"

"Not possible. You have to unscrew this see? It's even child-proof. As a matter of fact, it has to be on some trips."

She seemed fascinated by the rockets, and asked more questions before she could be led away. Next, he took her amid-ships, to the dining room, various bars, and finally the casino itself. It was a splendid room some fifty feet long by twenty wide, richly decorated in Eastern style, with carpeting so deep their feet sank an inch into it. Laura admired the chandeliers, the ornate pillars everything.

"Are you a gambler Mrs. Kilburn?"

"Within reason. A little chemmy sometimes. I'm not an addict, if that's what you mean."

"I think you will see some real gaming here tonight. Usually, it starts at about ten. It goes on most of the night. In fact, a couple of nights ago, some of the passengers had breakfast sent in."

"Rather out of my class I'm afraid. It must get awfully stuffy, everyone smoking and so on."

"Yes," agreed her escort. "But the chap who designed this knew what he was about. At sea, the normal thing to do to relieve a heavy atmosphere, is to open a few portholes. But at four or five in the morning this can be unwise. The air is very cold, often damp. You will notice every six feet or so just above eye level, those red silk squares?"

"Yes, I thought them quite effective."

"They are, but not in the way you mean. They are ventilators. A steady circulation of breathable air is kept moving in here at all times. The entire atmosphere is changed twice a minute. That's what I meant about the designer."

"Brilliant. How does it work?"

"Well if you're really interested," he said doubtfully. "It isn't much to see."

He took her to a small room not more

than six feet square, which lay behind the casino. She found it necessary to ask a number of seemingly pointless questions about the air exchange control. It was now six o'clock, and time was getting short.

"It's awfully good of you to have given up so much of your time," she gushed. "I mean, with all these passengers, I'm sure you're really terribly busy."

He laughed.

"Candidly, madam, that is one thing I cannot claim. The passenger complement of this vessel is over eight hundred, plus one hundred and five crew. This is a very special cruise indeed. We have only seventy passengers, and since there is a crew of fifty odd, we can hardly claim to be overworked. Confidentially, it's almost as much of a holiday for us as it is for you."

She did not let him take her quite to the cabin door. Already, there was the beginning of a familiar gleam in his eye, and that was definitely to be discouraged.

"Well thank you very much indeed,

Mr. Slater," she cooed.

"A pleasure madam, I do assure you. If there should be anything else while you're aboard?"

"I'll look for you at once," she promised.

At the cabin, she met Louise approaching from the opposite direction. They looked at Laura's wardrobe critically, and decided on the green silk. As she prepared herself, Laura chattered away to the girl. She was not employed by the Bey, it transpired, but counted as ship's staff. The Bey was a very grand person, as were the other oil princes aboard. There was little social life for them, outside of the casino. Each man preferred to remain with his own retinue, except for formal occasions, such as lunch and dinner. Many of them indeed, did not appear even for lunch, but had it served instead in their suites. There were few Westerners aboard, outside of the owner and his associates. The crew had a more social time altogether, having full use of what was normally the cabin class accommodation. Every night there was some activity for them, and tonight there was a dance. Occasionally, if some of the passengers felt like a change from the green baize covered tables, they would join in whatever the crew were doing. At night there were only a handful of people involved in the actual running of the ship, bridge and engine room staff mainly. Mr. Pasquale? Oh yes, a very nice man. Always genial and courteous with everyone. Some of his associates did not seem very good at mixing, keeping very much to themselves. It was evident Louise was having the time of her life.

"There, I think that will do?"

Laura turned from the mirror, the green of the dress seemed to set off the copper in her hair. Louise inspected her professionally.

"You are most beautiful, madame. There is something, something. Ah, I have it. No jewellery. Do you not think a pendant, perhaps, or rings for the ears?"

Laura shook her head.

"No. Perhaps later in the evening. Not now. Well thank you Louise. You've been most helpful. Now you can get off to your dancing."

"Oh, it will not commence before ten-thirty at least. We have to be certain the passengers are in the casino first. This is in case they should require something."

"Well," smiled Laura. "Perhaps I'll see you later."

"And the morning, madame? What will you wish?"

"That I cannot say. I do not know what the night will bring."

Louise smiled her understanding, and went out. Soon afterwards, Mr. Ulfrim appeared, looking more like a movie gangster than ever, in a cream dinner jacket and maroon bow tie. He eyed her with gratified appreciation.

"Madame, you are exquisite. His Eminence will be most pleased."

"With me, or with you?" she couldn't resist asking.

"With both of us, I trust. If you are quite ready?"

She accompanied him through the maze of corridors, pausing at last outside what seemed like the door of an ordinary cabin. A quiet tap, and a large Arab opened the door. He was splendid, in a flowing white gown with a jewelled scimitar at his waist.

"Ah Raschid," greeted Ulfrim, then followed with a burst of Arabic. The big man opened the door wide, bowing as Laura made her entrance. It was no ordinary cabin, but a huge room furnished with more regard to expense than taste. The aroma of conflicting perfumes was heavy on the air.

Several people, mostly in Eastern dress, were gathered about a man who sat on a mauve silken divan. All turned to look at her, and among the varied expressions on the men's faces, Laura could not find one of disappointment. Ulfrim ushered her across to the seated man.

"Your Eminence," he fawned, "I have the honour to present Mrs. Kilburn."

From beneath heavy lids, the Bey of Damasha looked at his latest acquisition. Yes, good. Really very good. Clever little devil, Ulfrim. Untrustworthy, but clever. Everyone waited expectantly for his decision. There was a noticeable easing of tension when he finally extended his hand.

"So glad you could come, Mrs. Kilburn. Won't you please sit?"

There was nowhere close by that she could sit, except next to the great man himself. She hesitated, then caught Ulfrim's eye, who gave a slight nod. Then she sat beside his master, who turned to look at her more closely.

"As a son of the true faith, I am not permitted alcohol. But I do not ignore the customs of my Western friends. Please take something."

A man stood before her.

"Thank you. Martini please. Dry. Two olives."

The man went away. There was something on the Bey's face that could have been approval. This woman knew what she wanted. Very well, that made two of a kind. He began to talk to her, and as he did so, the others talked among themselves. It was all very much as Laura had imagined the European courts must have been in medieval times. She found the man interesting. He had been to England several times, and was a great follower of football and the theatre. Laura could not contribute very much about football, but the theatre was familiar ground. It was easy to talk to him, and there was no reference by either of them to the reason for her presence.

"It has been most enjoyable, Mrs. Kilburn. And now you must excuse me. I dine at nine, if that is convenient."

She was being dismissed. As she got up, Ulfrim materialized beside her.

"I will see you to your cabin, madame."

As they walked back, the little man was jubilant.

"You have impressed my master most favourably. Oh yes, most favourably indeed."

He was practically rubbing his hands. Laura smiled slightly.

"So glad you approve. Will you call for me at nine?"

"At five minutes before, if you please."

Back in the cabin, Laura checked quickly to see if anything had been disturbed. There was no sign of interference, and the lid of the cistern was as she had left it. With an hour to pass before dinner, she thought about another trip on deck, decided against it. She could not afford to appear too interested in the ship's workings, and for another thing the evening breeze would not help her carefully prepared hair. Instead, she spent the time concentrating on what she had learned, and the use to which she had to put her information. Timing, as always, was vital. There were gaps in her knowledge, gaps which had to be filled before the time came to act.

She was deep in thought when the knock came at the door. Good Lord, it was already five to nine. Ulfrim stood smiling, and holding out a small velvet cushion.

"His Eminence trusts you will do him the honour."

Her eyes widened at the sight of the sparkling pendant, with the huge ruby. Taking it carefully, she held it against her throat, turning her face this way and that, studying the effect.

"His Eminence need have no fear on that score," she assured Ulfrim. "It's quite beautiful."

She let him fasten it, her eyes fascinated

by the reflection of the stone in the mirror. She had never worn anything so perfect.

"Come, I must thank your master."

"I am sure you will, madame."

It was a fair enough comment to the woman she was supposed to be, and Laura bit back the angry retort which rose to her lips. The Bey was now wearing a white silken tunic suit, with emeralds at his throat, and on the cuffs. He cut off her thanks quickly.

"Such a stone is nothing, till worn by an exquisite woman," he assured her, "Come, you must be ready to eat."

They made an impressive entrance into the dining-room, followed by the Bey's retinue, including Ulfrim. Conversation did not cease when they arrived, but Laura noted with satisfaction the covert looks from men and women alike. The Bey sat down first, motioning Laura to his right. Ulfrim and another man leaped to assist her with her chair. The table was aglitter with silver and crystal glass, set off by cloths of the snowiest white. In fact, Laura decided, glittering was the only adjective which did justice to the entire assembly. Rich silks, in the most exotic hues, were to be seen on all sides.

She was not consulted about the menu, the Bey ordering in quick precise terms. Mentally, she had made a pact with herself to eat sparingly. One look at the baby soles fried in bread-crumbs, and Laura was lost. The Bey watched approvingly as she made her way steadily through course after course.

"You eat well. That is good. Women who pick at their food annoy me."

If not exactly a compliment, it was at least a favourable comment.

"Everything is so delicious," she replied.

It was past ten when they were toying with the thick Turkish coffee. Laura had declined brandy. Her head would need to be absolutely clear later that night.

"Do you gamble, Mrs. Kilburn?" asked the great man.

"Not really," she denied. "A little occasional flutter nothing more."

"I gamble heavily, and to win. I normally commence at eleven and play all night. However, in honour of my charming guest, I feel I ought not to play too long. Would it bore you if I played until, shall we say, three o'clock? The sacrifice on my part is, I promise you, great."

Not so great, imagined, Laura as the sacrifice she was expected to make after three o'clock.

"As you wish," she murmured. "I feel guilty about taking you away from your game."

His eyes flashed with quick humour.

"I am sure it will be a matter of small regret on this occasion."

Their conversation was interrupted by the approach of a small dapper man in his late middle age.

"Ah, your Eminence, everything is the way you want it, I hope?"

He had the flat nasal twang of the New Yorker.

"Everything is satisfactory. I believe you have not met my guest. Mrs. Kilburn this is Mr. Pasquale. Sometime of America, now back in his native Italy."

She didn't offer to shake hands. It was all she could manage to keep the hatred from her face as she looked at the man who had ordered John's murder.

"Nice to meet you, Mrs. Kilburn. You British?"

"Yes. But I've been to New York."

His face clouded.

"Zasso? Well, that is one fine city. I'll probably see you later, at the tables."

The Bey had been watching this passage between them.

"You do not like him. Why?"

"Do you know who he is, your Mr. Pasquale?"

"Some kind of criminal, or so I am told. But that is not my concern. He has organized an extremely good cruise here. No publicity, indeed no public worth speaking of. My — what is it you call us — oh, yes, tycoons. My brother tycoons and I can relax in complete freedom and complete safety. That is what Mr. Pasquale has arranged for us, and that is very much my concern."

The dining-room was thinning out now, as small parties rose and made their various stately exits.

"Come, it is almost eleven. Tonight I

feel lucky." Then chuckling at his own little joke, he looked into Laura's eyes. "Indeed, on reflection, whether or not I win at the tables, tonight I am lucky."

Laura flushed and that seemed to please him, too.

The casino was busy when they arrived. The Bey stood at the entrance, looking at the scene with evident content. When he snapped his fingers, one of his attendants came forward and handed him a light brown pigskin wallet. This he opened, and Laura hoped her eyes didn't widen too much at the sight of so much money. The Bey riffled at the notes, extracting a thick wad.

"Five thousand," he stated. "And two-fifty more."

The attendant wrote this down carefully, and the Bey returned the wallet.

"Madame, you will do me an honour by being my lucky charm for the evening." He handled her the smaller packet of notes. "There you will find two hundred and fifty dollars. Please play with it as you will. Should you be unlucky, there will be more."

"Cash?" queried Laura. "Surely, with such people as yourself and these other princes, it would be safer to use cheques? It seems awfully dangerous to have so much cash aboard."

He considered this, smiling.

"But cheques, my dear lady, mean banks. They mean all kinds of records, book-keeping. Too many people become involved, too many people know. Next to gold, cash is much the best thing. One bets, one wins or loses, cash changes hands. It is finished. There are always those who seek to know of such things for political reasons. Cheques are an open invitation to such people. As to danger, what danger can there be here? We are all together, all for the same purpose."

"And that man, the gangster Pasquale? You think he is to be trusted?"

A short laugh was the immediate response.

"Trusted? I am completely certain he cannot be trusted. But he is also not a fool. This little affair provides rich pickings for him. He does not need to steal as well. And even if he considered it, he would reject the thought. We are powerful men, all of us. He would have a very short time in which to enjoy the proceeds. Come now, enough of this, you are in no danger, and tonight you are rich. Let us begin."

There was not even a grille on the cashier's desk. The Bey and Laura purchased their chips and the small dark man behind the counter looked with quick amusement at the size of her funds.

"Only one favour I ask, Mrs. Kilburn. Please do not play at my table. You may watch whenever you like, but do not take part."

"Very well. I will see you later."

He looked at her to see whether there was any second meaning behind that, then nodded heavily and strode towards a centre table. The others accompanied him, except Ulfrim, who seemed to have been given the job of escorting her. She went round the smaller tables at the sides of the room, knowing that she could not afford the centre games. The lowest minimum stake she could find was a twenty dollar game of vingt-et-un.

"Well, this appears to be about my bracket," she told Ulfrim. "Are you going to play?"

"Alas, I am a poor man. But I shall enjoy to watch, if you do not mind."

She lost the first two games, won the third. After that she lost twice more, then won seven games one after the other. With an occasional loss, she continued to win steadily. At mid-night, she had won nine hundred dollars. Laura had been interested primarily in passing time and it was with some surprise she realized having become so engrossed in the play that she had not noticed the clock. Occasionally, other players had joined in for a hand or two, but it was mainly by way of enjoying a break from the real action on the big tables. Laura was the only steady player. Ulfrim had sat quietly beside her, making no sound, and smoking endless fat Turkish cigarettes.

"Look at the time," she exclaimed, "it's five minutes past midnight."

"Time is of no importance here, madame," replied Ulfrim. "And you

338

seem to have used it well."

"Yes, I've been lucky haven't I? Perhaps a break for a little while."

She told the dealer she would probably be back, and got up.

"Where is your master playing?"

"He is on the second roulette table. That one."

The place was very busy now, and Laura surmised that everyone was present. Ulfrim led her to a spot behind the Bey of Damasha. Every seat was filled, and Laura tried to make a mental count of the piles of chips in the numbered squares, but quickly gave up. Ulfrim whispered to one of the Bey's retinue then turned to her.

"The master has lost tonight. Seventy-two thousand dollars so far."

Laura heard this in silence, watching the little white ball bouncing about on the wheel in the centre.

"Trente cinq. Noir."

There was a momentary laxing of tension, while the croupier pushed piles of chips in various directions. Then the next bets were made, and the wheel resumed its spinning. Laura and Ulfrim watched for about twenty minutes, by which time the Bey had lost another seven thousand.

"I'm not bringing him any luck," she whispered. "Let's move away."

Clear of the table, she wondered whether she ought to shake free of Ulfrim, decided it might look suspicious.

"The ship's staff are having a dance down below," she told him. "Could we go down and have a look?"

"If it would amuse you," he shrugged.

As they went out she saw Pasquale by the cashier's booth. He nodded coolly, and she ignored him. Two of his so-called associates lingered by the door. Their suits had evidently been specially tailored, because there was no sign of the guns she knew they must be carrying. Ulfrim opened the heavy glass doors for her to pass through. They hissed back together, completing the air lock without which the atmosphere exchange equipment could not operate.

The night air was chilly, and Laura rubbed her arms.

"Can I get you a coat, madame?"

"No thank you, it's rather refreshing. I think it's this way."

The staff dance was in full swing. No one paid any special attention to the new arrivals. Laura spotted Louise, in the rapturous clasp of a huge man in a steward's uniform, and smiled at they swung past. The atmosphere was heavy, and thick with tobacco smoke and alcohol fumes. No special airconditioning here. They had some coffee, and watched the dancing for a while.

"I regret I am not at all proficient at these gymnastics. However if madame wishes to — ?"

"No it's all right, thank you. I was only curious to have a look. I'd like to leave now."

On the way out she looked for Louise.

"Ah madame, it is a splendid party, no?"

"It certainly seems to be going well, Louise. It seems a pity for it to end."

"End? Oh no, madame. There is no rule about this. We shall continue for many hours yet."

"Lucky you. Have a good time. I'll see you tomorrow."

"Good night, madame."

It was almost one o'clock, and Laura felt an anticipatory shiver. At one-fifteen, she had some work to do.

18

She told Ulfrim she wanted to freshen up in her cabin.

"Please go back to the casino," she told him. "I'd feel guilty leaving you hanging about in this night air. I shall only be about half-an-hour."

The little man did not need much persuasion. Laura watched him go, then followed, until she saw him disappear through the casino doors. At once, she made her way down to the cabin, locking the door carefully. From this point on, there could be no turning back. If things did not go as they were intended, it would be too late for her to cover up.

Removing the lid from the cistern, she quickly ripped off the tape. From her recent training, she immediately checked the mechanism of the little .25 automatic, and found it in perfect order. Quickly, she removed her clothes, and undid the parcel. The familiar black overalls were cold against her skin, but at least she was now herself, Laura Kilburn. That other one, the calculating so-called woman of the world, had never been better than a stranger to her. A final adjustment to the belt, and she was ready for the other contents, a shining black gas mask, and half a dozen small round objects. Carefully she slid the respirator over her head, tightening the side straps the way she'd been shown. Most unbecoming, she decided. The automatic went into one pocket, the plastic balls into the other. Now she was ready. According to her watch it was ten minutes past one. A last look round the cabin, and she looked longingly at the ruby pendant, lying on the small dressing table. Impulsively, she scooped it up, and dropped it into her breast pocket.

Outside, the corridor was empty. She made her way rapidly and silently up on deck, checking carefully to ensure there were no late night strollers. Timing was everything now, and she found her heart beating unmercifully loudly. She knew exactly what she had to do, and how to do it. The only unpredictable factor was discovery. Hugging the ship's rail, she moved swiftly to the stern. There was no one there. Kneeling, she dismantled the safety mechanism on the big signal rockets, glancing continually over her shoulder as she did so. Ready. A quick check showed the time to be one-fourteen. Sixty seconds ticked away with agonizing slowness. Now. She fired one rocket, two, that was the signal. As fast as she could, she made her way back amid-ships. The rockets had sounded in the still night like a battery of field guns. Someone must have heard them. Running feet now, heavy on the wooden deck. Laura flattened herself against a lifeboat, as a man came into view. He was moving fast, and there was a large black revolver in his hand. It was one of Pasquale's associates, and the gun was not there for ornament.

As he drew level, Laura kicked out at his knee, and at the same time brought both hands down in a vicious chop at the sides of his neck. He went down with one strangled grunt. The gun lay beside him.

Stooping, she swept it up and hurled it out to sea in a high curving arc. As she bent to the unconscious man, she heard someone else coming. There was no cover to be had, so she grabbed the side of the lifeboat and swung easily up and over. The second man had a gun, too, and he wasn't running.

"Hey George, is that you?"

Laura saw him pause uncertainly as he saw the sprawled figure on the deck. If he would only come up close, she prayed, he would be level with her, and she could leap on him. But the noise, that was something she could not afford.

Slowly, the man approached, another of Pasquale's thugs.

"George, what happened?"

He stared about him continually, alert for anyone in hiding. Laura congratulated herself on the choice of place. She could see his face clearly as he waited beside the prostrate George. There was doubt and suspicion there, writ large. She would have to spring, noise or no noise. She pushed her hands down to tense herself for the effort. Her right hand touched something hard. Of course, the fire extinguisher. A final check in all directions, and the man bent over George, turning the head round. The fire extinguisher hit him squarely on the back of the head, and he slumped forward, losing hold of the revolver. Then Laura was on him, with a hard jolt behind the ear to finish him off. These two ought really to be tied up, but there was no time. Already she'd lost precious minutes, and others may come looking for them. She sent the second gun to join its fellow in the Mediterranean and made for the casino. Avoiding the lighted deck area outside the doors, she ran for the room containing the temperature controls. Inside, it took her seconds only to jam the mechanism. Whatever air there was inside the casino would have to last them a while. The next part was probably the most dangerous in the whole cruise. She found herself trembling with the same kind of exultant fear she'd known before, and was coming to recognize.

When she drew close to the entrance,

Laura moved gingerly, a foot at a time. She had already decided the best way to tackle this part of it. Everything inside was as she had left it. Evidently, the players had had no idea of what was going on outside. Pasquale would see to that, she thought grimly.

The two guards inside the entrance were talking together. Their backs were to her, which was fortunate for them. Taking the .25 from her pocket, she disengaged the safety catch. A deep breath, and she ran to the glass doors, pulling one quickly open and stepped inside. The two men swung round to see who was coming in, their faces going slack with astonishment at the sight of the black-clad figure with a gas mask for a face. But the gun was familiar enough. One man dived into his pocket. She shot him in the shoulder, and he went down cursing. The other man slowly raised his hands. The sound of the shot brought people's eyes to the doorway, but Laura had no time to concern herself with them now. Taking one of the plastic balls from her pocket, she flung it against the wall.

348

Then a second, and the third she flung up to the ceiling in the middle of the room. Clouds of vapour drifted quickly into the atmosphere. It was time to go, but she could not leave the second guard with a gun. A few bullet holes in the glass door might permit too much gas to escape. Motioning him to turn round, she hit him expertly and watched him go down. There was panic now, people shouting and running for the doors. She fired a warning shot into the carpet, and they stopped where they were. Now she stepped quickly outside, swinging the sealed glass door heavily into place. She stood there, just a few feet away from them, holding the gun where they could see it.

The whole thing was over in seconds. One man reached for his collar as though to loosen his tie. Then, as if in a slow motion film, he pitched gradually forward to the floor. People began to drop where they stood. At the tables, players simply sagged over the green tops. It was an amazing sight, and not one she enjoyed very much.

She allowed a full half-minute, twice the time allotted for the guaranteed results. As a last precaution, she removed an oar from the nearest lifeboat, and inserted it across the joined handles of the doors. Probably unnecessary, she admitted to herself. Now, she ran, not attempting to hide, down to the cabin-class saloon, where the staff were having their party. From earlier checks, she knew there were two other side doors apart from the main entrance, each leading to small service rooms which did duty as bars and for storage, etc. The first one was easy. The room was in darkness, and all she had to do was open the door, remove the key from the inside, and lock it quickly. She threw the key away and moved round to the next door. It opened easily enough, but then it was difficult to tell who was the more surprised Laura, who almost fell into a couple who had decided there was more to life than dancing, or the couple, faced with this bleak apparition. The man recovered first.

"Hey, what the devil are you — ?"

Laura put a finger to her mouth for

silence and nodded towards the salon, where, if noise was any indication, living was high. The man grinned understandingly.

"Oh some sort of game, eh? All right, we'll keep quiet."

His companion wagged her head vigorously. Laura saluted gravely, quietly removing the key behind her back. Then she moved swiftly back, slamming the door shut and inserting the key, just as the man leaped forward and began to bang on the panels. Too close she admitted, as she flipped the key into the darkness. Running round to the main entrance, she almost collided with a man weaving an unsteady path along the corridor. Uncertain what to do to this perfectly harmless individual, she paused. He looked at her, blinked owlishly, then grinned a wide vacant grin. "Jolly good," he said, in English. "Jolly good." A friendly slap on her shoulder, and he went on his way. Laura sighed with relief. At the main doors now, she opened them just far enough to be able to peer in. The atmosphere was thick, the noise

351

deafening. She flipped one of the small gas bombs hard against the opposite wall, then another. No one noticed at first, then one or two shouts came through the doors. But there was such confusion inside already and so much din, it was only a few of those nearest to the doors who realized the danger. In panic, they rushed to get out, but the emergency fire axe wedged across the handles was too much for them. Soon there was no sound, other than the raucous music from the record-player. Laura checked the time, and found it was one-thirty-five. She'd taken a couple of minutes longer to reach this stage than had been intended. It was time for the second signal.

Hurrying back up on deck, she made her way to the stern. George and the other man were still as she had left them. A few seconds, and the other two signal rockets roared up into the darkness. Laura watched the brilliant trails with relief. The arrangement had been that if the operation was possible that night she would release two rockets. She would then do what had to be done,

352

and the second signal would be sent up not more than thirty minutes after the first. If the second signal was not made within that time, it would mean that something had gone wrong, and the raid was off. Now, watching the soaring red lines, she knew she would not be alone for long. They had promised to land not more than five minutes after the clearance signal. That meant they were up there somewhere. She strained her ears for the sound of engines but could hear nothing. Little doubts came into her mind, despite herself. One minute went by, two. No engines. Fretting, she went again to check on George and the other man, just in time to see George stir and begin to moan. She put him back to sleep, looked at her watch for the tenth time. Three minutes gone. She ought to be hearing something by now. Helicopter engines were not exactly the most timid in the air. But still there was nothing but the gentle motion of the sea, as it splashed against the sides of the liner.

Acutely conscious of the need for help

now, Laura kept searching the deck area for signs of attack. The people on the bridge must know something was going on, and it was hard to believe that only two of Pasquale's men were on patrol. She had gone beyond the point of no return, and would be bound to face a situation at any moment with which she could not cope.

Now there was a sound, a great hissing sound that was somehow familiar. A dark shape loomed up from the night, just to her right, and now she realized what it was. An enormous glider was rushing on to the water, not twenty yards from the ship. That was why she had heard nothing before. Running to the side she began waving furiously. Small rubber dinghies appeared beside the black glider, and moved steadily towards her. As the first reached the side of the ship a voice called:

"Stand well back."

A weighted line snaked over the rail, slithered, then held fast. Then another, and another. Soon a black figure, wearing a respirator like her own clambered over the side. A man's voice, hollow and distorted said:

"Everything O.K.?"

She nodded. Others quickly joined them. Already there were eight in the party, and more coming. The leader motioned her to lead the way, and she went off at a trot to the silent casino. One man lifted away the oar which had done duty as a bolt, then they opened the door and went in. Inside, they paused at the astonishing sight of so many people apparently hopelessly drunk. They were sprawled in every conceivable position, out to the world. The leader tapped another man on the shoulder, who immediately pulled off his respirator. A few deep breaths, and he nodded.

"Okay."

The leader took off his own mask, and so did the others, Laura was one of the last. She'd seen what the gas could do, and didn't want any first-hand experience of it. Reluctantly, she slid the straps over her head, and took a cautious sniff. Then she saw Nagumi, who smiled at her and nodded. She was pleased by the approval.

"What about the rest, Mrs. Kilburn?"

Quickly, she told them what had happened so far.

"But there must be some others about," she emphasized. "I couldn't have had that much luck."

"Right. Khan, take three men and search. Be careful before you shoot. Most of these are ordinary people."

The brown-skinned Khan nodded, and left with the others. The leader spoke to the rest of them.

"We have not less than twenty minutes, not more than thirty. You know what to do. Leave nothing."

Each man carried a small sack made of oiled skin. They moved into the casino, taking everything of value and stowing it in the sacks.

"The real money, I fancy, will be in there?"

The leader pointed to the small booth which served as the cashier's desk. Laura nodded.

"Then let's see what we have."

He kicked open the locked door at the side and they went in. Below the counter was more money than Laura had ever seen in her life. Neat rectangular piles, stacked close together.

"No."

He stopped her as she was about to put a pile into the sack in his hands.

"On the counter, please. I want to get a rough idea of how much there is."

It seemed like a spending of unnecessary time to Laura. As quickly as they could, they began to count. A pile of hundred dollar bills came to ten thousand. Laura picked up the next pile, and began again.

"No, not like that. This is ten thousand?"

Laura nodded. Surely he wasn't actually going to check. But she need not have worried.

"Here's what we do. Take another pile, as near as you can the same height, of the same denomination. See? If that's ten, so is this, give or take a few hundred."

It made good sense. In no time they had completed the count. Before them on the counter was almost half-a-million dollars.

"Half-a-million," she echoed dis-believingly.

"Give or take a few," he reminded. "That's why I wanted to check. It's not enough."

"Not enough?" she found herself repeating, in wonder.

"No. There's a lot more somewhere. Is there a strong room, or something like that?"

"I don't know," she admitted. "There's bound to be some kind of safe in the purser's office."

"That's it. We'll try there. Come on."

She led him to the square where there were the usual ship's shops. The purser's office lay to one side, and the door was locked. The man stepped back and fired one shot into the lock, then kicked the door open. The safe was built into the side of the office, and was unlike any Laura had seen before. The leader groaned.

"Just our luck. A Barker and Mulloy. Nip back and ask for Chang, then bring him here."

Laura went back to the casino where

the others were about half-finished.

Chang was a large, good-tempered Chinese, who nodded understandingly and followed her back.

"What do you make of it, Chang?"

"Barker and Mulloy," announced Chang. "Pittsburgh company. Best in business. Very tough."

"Can it be done?"

"Yes. But take all night."

He looked questioningly at the leader, who thought for only a moment.

"All right. You'll have to use that damned stuff of yours. Try not to kill yourself. At least until the safe is open."

"The lady will please leave."

He produced a small box from his overall pocket, as Laura went back outside. The leader soon joined her.

"Genius, that chap," he said chattily. "You'll see. Keep clear of the door."

Seconds later, Chang emerged from the open door. Or, more accurately, catapulted himself through it in a flying tackle. As he hit the deck there was a high-pitched noise from within, then a loud explosion. Pieces of wood flew out, some landing on the prostrate Chinese.

"No, please." He held up a hand as he got to his feet. "I check."

He went into the clouds of smoke, and was soon out again.

"You see," he invited. "Most lovely sight in all world."

Eyes stinging from the smoke they went to the safe.

"Yes," breathed the leader. "A lovely sight. Better than I expected."

Bank notes from a dozen countries were heaped neatly on the shelves. Except for the bottom compartment.

"Is that what I think it is?" asked Laura, pointing.

"It is. Bullion, my dear. Pure gold. This is quite a find. Chang, ask a couple of the chaps to come and give a hand."

They got to work emptying the shelves. Others came to help, and Laura was surprised to note that one gold bar at a time was enough for one man to carry. Every one was cheerful as they went on deck and began lowering the bags down to the men in the rubber dinghies below. It had all taken time, and Laura now looked at her watch.

"The gas will be wearing off soon, won't it?"

She was working alongside Nagumi at that moment. He turned.

"In about ten minutes, yes. Why?"

"Shall we be finished in time?"

"Probably. In any case, these people will give no trouble. The boys will have taken any arms they were carrying."

There was a noisy rattle somewhere along the deck. Nagumi shouted and grabbed his arm. Blood welled between his fingers. Instinctively, Laura dropped to the boards, pulling him down. Beside them, another man clawed at his chest and gave a high scream. There was nothing Laura could do to prevent it as he arched back over the rail and tumbled out of sight towards the sea.

Looking round, Laura could see three others besides Nagumi and herself, all low on the deck.

"Where's the gun?" she called softly.

"Don't know," replied one man. "Had our backs to him when he let go."

"How many of our people have finished

so far?" asked Nagumi in evident pain.

"A lot have gone back. The casino was finished. Probably one or two left amidships, and we five here. Say seven."

"It should have been eight," chimed in another, in a thick guttural accent.

"Yes. Who was it went over the side?" Nagumi wanted to know.

"Nikki. I think he's had it. Nagumi you're the senior operator here. What do we do?"

Nagumi's head sank on to his chest. Laura, afraid he was going to pass out, shook him by the shoulder. He jerked upright again.

"Is there a number three here?"

"Yes," answered one. "I'm number three."

"Still got your signal torch?"

"Yes."

"Right. The first thing is to prevent a rescue act from the glider. The comedian with the stutter-gun would pick them off like a kid in a penny arcade as they came over that rail. Get a keep out signal flashing. Keep doing it till they acknowledge."

The man rolled to the side, gaining what protection he could from the life raft lashed there, and went to work with the torch.

"What about the rest of us?" demanded another. "We just can't stay here all night. For one thing, these people could be creeping up on us for all we can tell. I don't fancy lying here just waiting to be butchered."

"Vraiment," said his companion. "Also, we must consider the passengers. Soon they will emerge, and then maybe innocent get hurt, I think."

He was right. Laura had a fleeting mental vision of a gun-fight while harmless, gas-stupefied, passengers stumbled about the deck. The picture was not pleasant.

"We must know where they are," decided the Japanese. "I need a volunteer to make them shoot again. I cannot go myself."

They all offered, but it was Laura who spoke first.

"You are a woman," objected the Frenchman.

"That is an offensive remark," Laura

told him coldly. "I'm as good as any of you, and you know it. Besides, if they should catch me they'd be less likely to kill me out of hand. That would be an unnecessary waste, the way these thugs' minds work."

"Good enough for me. She has the job," Nagumi approved. "The rest of us will each watch a different part of the ship, spot where the fire comes from. No, Mrs. Kilburn, not yet."

She paused, surprised.

"First I must know about the glider," he explained.

They fell silent. It was eerie, lying full-length on the now-chill boarding, while the sea-sounds came to them faintly. Now and then, Nagumi stirred painfully, and Laura wished there was something she could do for him. Suddenly he whispered.

"By the way, don't forget there are probably a couple of our people around. Don't start blasting at everything that moves."

"I'll remember."

Movement now, as the signaller inched back to them.

"O.K. Nagumi, they acknowledge."

"Good. Ready, Mrs. Kilburn?"

"Ready."

Her heart began that thumping again. "Then go."

She leaped to her feet and ran. A twisting, dodging movement aimed for the protection of the aft hatch covers. She had covered a dozen feet before she heard the gun again, this time joined by another. But she was fully exposed and there was nothing to do but carry on. Things, that sounded like bees on a summer afternoon, zipped around her in the semi-darkness. She jumped the last six feet, clutching fervently at the wondrous solidity of the comforting wood. The guns stopped. The fear was dominated now by anger. Anger at these people of Pasquale's, who would casually snuff out her life this way, like a beetle on a wall. Well, maybe they wouldn't have things quite so much their own way from this point on. The firing had come from her right, and that meant they were up close by the casino, since there was no cover for them in between. The question was, which side? They could be amidships, where there were plenty of shields for them, or on the other side, between the casino and the rail where there were lifeboats and other paraphernalia to hide them. One satisfaction was she was no longer restricted. She could work her way around the hatch covers and see how things looked from the other side. Gently, she edged towards the stern, each foot taking her further from the guns. One step now, and she would round the angle, and be sheltered completely. Thankfully, she slid round the corner.

And found herself face to face with a man.

There was no time or discussion about which was the most surprised. The man's dark Italian face went slack with astonishment. Her own probably looked no better. Laura's instincts were sharper. There could be many reasons. She had been living on the edge of death for twenty-four hours. He had been softened by two weeks of casual, seemingly unnecessary duty. There was nothing casual about the gun in his hand, a large blue-black revolver, gleaming faintly with oil. Nothing casual either, about Laura's reaction. The gun had started at his side, pointing down. He swung it up and forward as fast as he could. But Laura had been moving before he stopped gasping. Her right foot was lashing into his groin before the gun was at right angles. His anguished curse was cut short by the pointed elbow which jabbed mercilessly into his throat. He swung the gun hard, but the damned woman was no longer there. She was inside his arm, back pressing against him. Again, that elbow, like an arrow into his middle, and as he tried to bend, to alleviate the sharp, shooting agony inside, he found himself sailing forward, the deck rising towards his face. Laura, automatically tensing herself to spring on him as he landed, held back. The guns spoke in the night. She recoiled both in horror and in safety reflex, as the man on the deck twisted and cavorted as lead smashed into him. Sweat ran down her face, and she brushed at it with an impatient arm. No point in standing there. She would have had to kill him anyway. And the bullets had been intended for her. That was the reason, the real reason, why she was trembling so. That was meant to be her life, oozing slowly out on to the scrubbed boards, making a widening stain. Her resolve had been high before. Now it was at absolute altitude.

The encounter had been too close, and she had not been ready. Not really ready. The .25 was still tucked away in her pocket, where it could do nobody any harm. Doing harm, to somebody, was getting to be a dominating factor in this exercise. She slid her hand into her pocket, fondled the familiar little gun, then stopped. In her mind the voice of Haroun, her weapon instructor, was intoning monotonously. "It is a very good weapon, Mrs. Kilburn. In the right circumstances. But what are the right circumstances? I mean, look at that target."

"I am looking at it."

"You have made a good score. On a target."

She recalled getting impatient.

"And? A man would be bigger, surely?"

"Indeed. Bigger, indeed. But also human. Able to move, for one thing. Able to absorb pain for another. One has to consider fire-power."

And he had droned on. A shot from a .25 could kill a man. Would kill a man, at close range, and in perfect conditions. So could a .22, for that matter a .18. But for stopping power, for sheer muscle tearing, bone shattering, stop the bull dead in its tracks pain, a heavier calibre was required.

"I don't see — "

"Mrs. Kilburn, do not interrupt. Guns, I have told you before, are pieces of machinery. Let us take a simple case of sabotage. You wish to prevent a warship leaving harbour. A tiny piece of metal in the right place, let us say for comparison like the .25 or .22, will do the job. But you have no time. Or conditions are not appropriate. What is the alternative? Please, do not bother to answer. I see, by your face, you understand me. You take the biggest piece of equipment you can find, a four inch spanner, a fireman's axe, and you break something, anything. But it works. You take my parable. The first is for the expert, in ideal surroundings, in ideal circumstances. The second is for the real operative, desperate, human, but determined to achieve the end. Somehow, however crude the method, he will achieve the end."

"And the method is really a .45 heavy calibre?"

"If available," shrugged Haroun.

And it was available. There, not eight feet from where she stood. A lovely, heavy .45. Close by the feet of the dead man, and in full view of those guns. It was worth a risk to get it, but not worth her life. Looking round, she saw a life belt and had an idea. Lifting it from the hook, she took careful aim and wheeled it out into the light fast, and away from the corpse. The deadly rattle began at once, but she was already moving. In the two or three seconds between the gunman identifying the moving object and switching their attention back, she had the gun and was diving full-length for cover again. Panting, more from excitement than exertion, she stroked it fondly. A quick check was enough to ensure that it was loaded, and in good order. The man on the deck had not been an amateur.

Safe, behind the aft deck structure, she prowled around, hoping to find something that would help her resolve the problem of the men by the casino. A minute was sufficient to bring home the fact that no magic solution was to hand. Squatting down, she stared out at the luminous white trail that followed the ship, thinking hard. By her reasoning, there was a stalemate. Nagumi and the others were unable to move, because movement could only bring exposure to the machine guns. The gunners, on the other hand, were in a way pinned down themselves. They would know her people to be armed, and therefore they could not risk exposure either. The time element was on Pasquale's side. The gas would be wearing off and soon there would be many people stirring, passengers and crew alike. Once that happened, Nagumi and the others were finished. There was no sign of any activity by the other two men not accounted for, and that probably meant Pasquale had dealt with them.

Uncomfortable as the thought was, the only free agent, the only person in a position to do anything positive, was herself. Not that she could do much. In her own way, she was as pinned down as Nagumi, because Pasquale knew where she was. Her slight advantage lay in the fact that she had a few yards of free movement in either direction. Which meant, she admitted glumly, that she could either sit there and wait, like the others, or alternatively, she could jump over the side, unhindered. At the thought, she went and leaned on the rail, staring down at the churning foam. How far down was it? Thirty feet? Forty? She could not judge, and anyway it was idle speculation, when she ought to be doing something positive. Turning her back to the sea, she stared at the curving wooden rail, disappearing out of sight, and into view of the casino. If only she were at the other end of the rail, it would be a very different story. Then she snapped her fingers in excitement. That was it. That was the route. No, she could not walk along beside the rail, an open invitation to the stuttering lead. But could she walk along underneath it? Kneeling quickly, she examined the rail. It was of conventional design. Metal uprights every so many yards, with protective barred railing between. The lowest cross-bar, the one to prevent unwary children and household pets from disappearing over the side, was four inches above the deck. That was her ladder, her private roadway alongside the ship. And it was something which had to be done, without too much preliminary thought. If she thought about it, her nerve might fail.

Immediately, she swung over the handrail, not looking below, and lowered herself carefully to the bottom bar. There she hung, flat against the side of the ship, wrists bent awkwardly, because the bar was a few inches inboard. A few experimental flexings of shoulder and back muscles, and she essayed her first swing to the left. At once, she found herself slapped hard against the steel plates, the two guns in her lower pockets banging painfully into her legs. She all but lost her grip, and clung grimly on, furious with herself, and knowing what she had done wrong. She had not allowed for the ship's movement. Luckily the Matruh had been at the end of a roll when Laura moved, otherwise the sudden impact would certainly have flung her clear, and out there, somewhere in the disappearing wake. Now, the ship began to move away from her again, and she could progress. Left hand, right hand in, left hand, right hand in. Each swing took her about one foot along the rail. She had made about six feet in this way, when she felt the stern coming up to meet her again. This time she was watching. Putting both feet forward, she pushed against the advancing metal. This brought her clear of the full impact, and using her legs as shock absorbers, she was soon lying happily against the Matruh, this time with minimum physical pain. Time to go again. By the third roll, she had achieved about twenty feet, and was becoming quite expert. Even able to adjust to the change, when instead of back and forth, she found the side of the ship moving up and down. This meant she was now at the port side, and probably could have a clear view of the open decks if she went up. It also meant, if anyone had keen enough eyes, her hands were in full view of Pasquale's gunmen. But there was no time for fear. Her whole mind and body had to concentrate on the massive physical task in hand. Progress was becoming more difficult, and it wasn't because of any change in the circumstances. It was due solely to the immense strain on her bodily resources.

As she reckoned, she was now little better than halfway to her destination. Had there been any alternative she would have accepted it. But the alternative was death, whichever way she failed. She could either climb up on to the deck, with the inevitable result, or she could relieve her wrists and shoulders of this bonecracking work, and disappear into the sea.

She rested a moment, drawing what

comfort she could from the metal solidity of the ship's plates. Clinging there, a human speck in the Mediterranean night, she wondered briefly whether it mattered so much if Laura Kilburn died. Without John, her life was empty, in any case. Who would there be to mourn? A few friends, a quick tear at the graveside. Only there wouldn't even be a graveside. She would make just a tiny splash in the ocean. And it would be so easy, such a relief, to let go of that torturing rail, from which every muscle cried out for release. Rubbish. Self-pity. Self-indulgent rubbish. All right, perhaps it didn't matter so much if Laura Kilburn died. But if she did, what would become of the four trapped men on the other side of the ship? They would die, certainly. And Pasquale. The man who ordered John's murder, the great Frankie Packer. He would still be alive, unpunished, perhaps having other people's Johns killed. No. If she had to die, it would not be by way of a self-comforting suicide.

Her arms found new strength. The determination and resolve of her mind seemed to add salve to strained and aching muscles. Steadily, detached from the physical effort, she swung her way along the rail. Left hand, right hand in. Left hand, right hand in. Now the end was in sight, just a few feet away. She could tell, looking back along the stern, that she was now well within the protection of the forward superstructure. A brief rest, and she began the laborious climb upward.

As soon as her face was level with the deck, she scanned everything in sight. She could see no one, and was certain she was now behind the gunmen. Exultant, she clambered over the rail, patted it gratefully, and went silently to the cover of the main dining salon. Peering round the corner, she could see the casino clearly. As she looked, shadows moved suddenly, and became men. There were three of them, hunched down in the semi-gloom, watching the stern carefully. Laura hoisted the .45, glad of its company. The problem was, were there others? Out there somewhere, as yet undetected by her. Well, there was no time to waste.

Creeping softly to the protection of a ventilator shaft, she called out:

"Throw away the guns."

Someone swore. One of the men swung round towards the voice. In his hands was a light machine-gun, kicking and jumping as he turned. Laura shot him in the chest, and he went down writhing. A second man fired at her with a revolver. Without moving, she took aim and fired back. Once, twice. He clutched at his stomach and slumped down. The third man started running, anywhere, away from this angel of death. Out on to the deck, and firing as he went. From the stern, a number of guns spoke, as Nagumi and the others saw him coming. The man fell in mid-stride, sprawling drunkenly along the deck for several feet, before becoming still.

Laura went and stood in the light, where those at the aft end could see her. The Frenchman and the others came out of the shadows, cautiously at first, fearful of another hidden group. When there was no fire, they ran towards her, weaving and ducking as a precaution.

"Bravo, madame, these will not trouble us again."

The Frenchman waved his hand towards the late opposition. Laura nodded briefly, not wishing to dwell on what had happened.

"We ought to find the others, and get out as quick as we can," she said.

"This is what Nagumi says. We must hurry. Already the gas is wearing off."

"I know the ship's inside. You come with me, and the others can search up here. Remember, the people on the bridge are ordinary sailors."

She ran off into the first class cabin area, the Frenchman close behind. They traversed one corridor, then another, without success. At the end of the third corridor they saw something gleaming, projecting round a corner.

"It is a boot," decided the Frenchman.

Guns ready, they advanced, going faster when they saw he was right.

"We need search no more."

Face down in the carpet was Khan, a knife driven to the hilt between his shoulders. Further along lay another man, also dead. The Frenchman knelt beside the Indian, patting gently at his shoulder.

"We have done much together, this one and I," he said softly.

"I'm afraid we'll have to leave them," said Laura practically. "We can't endanger the glider. The time it would take — "

"I am not an amateur, madame," snapped the other angrily. "I know what we must do. Come."

He stood, and as he did so a gun barked. Twice. He coughed, shook his head, looked at Laura in surprise. Then he slumped down beside his dead friend.

"I can kill you too, lady. I will, if you don't drop the gun. Now."

Laura stared around, unable to see the killer. There was nowhere she could run, nowhere to hide. She tossed the .45 to the ground.

"Good. That's better. I can use you alive."

And there suddenly, was Pasquale. Only now he was more his old gangster self, more Frankie Packer. The tommy-gun looked at if it had been born with him, black and evil as himself.

380

"How many more, and where are they?" he demanded.

She stared at him surlily. He chuckled.

"Tough, ain't ya? Well, it doesn't matter. We only have to wait. That stuff you used, whatever it was, it ain't gonna last all night. You nearly had a good thing going here. Almost worked. I coulda used a dame like you in the old days. Say, I know you. You're the one was with-er-what's-his-name, the Bey of Damasha. Right?"

"Right."

"Yeah. You don't like me. Why? I never done nothing to you."

"You murdered my husband. And I'm going to kill you for it."

The words were flat and expressionless, but they wiped the confident grin from his face. He patted the Thompson.

"You ain't gonna kill nobody, lady. Not while I got this. Let's move on out, and find your friends. Turn around and move."

She turned, and began to walk away. She could hear him behind her, three or four feet away, too far for any ambitious attempt at the gun. In her pocket, the little .25 nudged impatiently at her thigh, but she'd have no time to use it before the Thompson cut her in two. Running footsteps now ahead of them. She was about to cry out, but the hard muzzle dug painfully into her back.

"Shut up. You know what this thing does to people?"

So she walked, hearing the footsteps draw nearer. There they were, coming round the end of the corridor, the two she'd left searching outside. She was flung to one side as Packer let go with the Thompson. Now. Her hand dug desperately into her pocket, pulling out the .25 in a quick, smooth movement. Packer must have seen her out of the corner of his eye, preoccupied as he was. The first shot smashed into the side of his temple, the next hit him above the ear. The tommy-gun was swinging round towards her, but already he was falling backwards. From the end of the passage came the bark of a heavy automatic. The slug took him in the throat, and a great torrent of blood came gushing out, as from a switched-on hose. His fingers tightened by reflex action, and the Thompson began to rain lead, but because of the angle of his fall, the bullets went up. Ripping into upper walls and the ceiling of the corridor, leaving great jagged tears. Laura was hunched against the wall, petrified at the sight of this blood-drenched monster, seemingly spitting death in his last throes.

Suddenly it was over. He lay on his back, knees bent under him, the sub-machine gun cradled obscenely across the now carmine chest.

"You all right, Mrs. Kilburn?" came an anxious shout.

Unable to speak, she nodded. Then straightening up, she stumbled towards the waiting men.

"Good thing you got him," said one. "We hadn't much chance against that thing."

She nodded again, wanting only to get out, away from this. One of them seemed to understand. Taking her by the arm, he propelled her gently up and into the night air.

"Time to go. Where are the others?"

"Dead. All dead," she muttered.

It was as though, with the death of Pasquale, all the life had been drained from her also. She stumbled up the steps, into the light.

"Hey, Laura. We haven't got all night, you know."

And there was Monahan, the Irish-American heathen, standing nonchalantly against the casino doors, grinning across at her.

"Monahan."

She went across to him, and he winked.

"Busy night, huh?"

"Yes," she agreed weakly. "You could put it that way."

"Can't hang around. Whole damned place'll be crawling with people in a few minutes."

"How did you get here?" she asked pointlessly.

"Been here all the time. On the glider. When you didn't show, I thought I'd better kind of look into it."

He looked away awkwardly. Laura squeezed his arm.

"Thank you."

"We can talk later. Come on."

"Just a minute. One thing I must do."

She darted into the casino. People were beginning to moan and stir.

"Damon Runyon would have loved this," said Monahan, beside her. "The biggest floating crap game in the world."

Laura went to where the Bey of Damasha was sitting, spread-eagled on the green baize, broken piles of blue chips by his out-stretched arms.

"What are you doing? What is that thing?"

"A present. I'd hate him to think I cheated him."

Forcing open his fingers, she took one last longing look at the ruby pendant, then placed it in his palm. In his other hand she put a sheaf of ten dollar bills.

"Two hundred and fifty dollars," she announced. "That was my stake money."

Monahan was puzzled by this seeming foolishness, but made no comment. Beside them, a man sat up, feeling tenderly at his throat.

385

"What — what is happening?" he asked weakly.

"Little trouble with the air supply," explained Monahan soothingly. "We have it fixed now. There'll be some coffee in a minute."

"Oh."

In his fuddled state, the passenger was in no mood to argue. Laura and Monahan went quickly outside.

"Time to go, honey. Can you dive?"

"Dive?"

She looked down at the gently moving water.

"It must be fifty feet," she protested.

"Forty is my guess. Come on."

He swung a leg over the handrail, and waited. Laura came over too. A hundred feet away, the big black glider rode easily on the waves.

"Jump well out, as far as you can. Here we go."

He held her hand. For a moment they stood there, poised in silhouette against the line of the Matruh. Laura closed her eyes. They jumped out, far out, and now she was falling. A wonderful sense of freedom and exhilaration filled her, as the night air rushed past her ears.

This is not the end, she thought contentedly.

This is only the beginning.

THE END

A FOOT IN THE GRAVE
Bruce Marshall

About to be imprisoned and tortured in Buenos Aires, John Smith escapes, only to become involved in an aeroplane hijacking.

DEAD TROUBLE
Martin Carroll

Trespassing brought Jennifer Denning more than she bargained for. She was totally unprepared for the violence which was to lie in her path.

HOURS TO KILL
Ursula Curtiss

Margaret went to New Mexico to look after her sick sister's rented house and felt a sharp edge of fear when the absent landlady arrived.

THE DEATH OF ABBE DIDIER
Richard Grayson

Inspector Gautier of the Sûreté investigates three crimes which are strangely connected.

NIGHTMARE TIME
Hugh Pentecost

Have the missing major and his wife met with foul play somewhere in the Beaumont Hotel, or is their disappearance a carefully planned step in an act of treason?

BLOOD WILL OUT
Margaret Carr

Why was the manor house so oddly familiar to Elinor Howard? Who would have guessed that a Sunday School outing could lead to murder?

THE DRACULA MURDERS
Philip Daniels

The Horror Ball was interrupted by a spectral figure who warned the merrymakers they were tampering with the unknown.

THE LADIES
OF LAMBTON GREEN
Liza Shepherd

Why did murdered Robin Colquhoun's picture pose such a threat to the ladies of Lambton Green?

CARNABY
AND THE GAOLBREAKERS
Peter N. Walker

Detective Sergeant James Aloysius Carnaby-King is sent to prison as bait. When he joins in an escape he is thrown headfirst into a vicious murder hunt.

MUD IN HIS EYE
Gerald Hammond

The harbourmaster's body is found mangled beneath Major Smyle's yacht. What is the sinister significance of the illicit oysters?

THE SCAVENGERS
Bill Knox

Among the masses of struggling fish in the *Tecta*'s nets was a larger, darker, ominously motionless form . . . the body of a skin diver.

DEATH IN ARCADY
Stella Phillips

Detective Inspector Matthew Furnival works unofficially with the local police when a brutal murder takes place in a caravan camp.

STORM CENTRE
Douglas Clark

Detective Chief Superintendent Masters, temporarily lecturing in a police staff college, finds there's more to the job than a few weeks relaxation in a rural setting.

THE MANUSCRIPT MURDERS
Roy Harley Lewis

Antiquarian bookseller Matthew Coll, acquires a rare 16th century manuscript. But when the Dutch professor who had discovered the journal is murdered, Coll begins to doubt its authenticity.

SHARENDEL
Margaret Carr

Ruth didn't want all that money. And she didn't want Aunt Cass to die. But at Sharendel things looked different. She began to wonder if she had a split personality.

1	21	41	61	81	101	121	141	161	181
2	22	42	62	82	102	122	142	162	182
3	23	43	63	83	103	123	143	163	183
4	24	44	64	84	104	124	144	164	184
5	25	45	65	85	105	125	145	165	185
6	26	46	66	86	106	126	146	166	186
7	27	47	67	87	107	127	147	167	187
8	28	48	68	88	108	128	148	168	188
9	29	49	69	89	109	129	149	169	189
10	30	50	70	90	110	130	150	170	190
11	31	51	71	91	111	131	151	171	191
12	32	52	72	92	112	132	152	172	192
13	33	53	73	93	113	133	153	173	193
14	34	54	74	94	114	134	154	174	194
15	35	55	75	95	115	135	155	175	195
16	36	56	76	96	116	136	156	176	196
17	37	57	77	97	117	137	157	177	197
18	38	58	78	98	118	138	158	178	198
19	(39)	59	79	99	119	139	159	179	199
20	40	60	80	100	120	140	160	180	200

201	216	231	246	261	276	291	306	321	336
202	217	232	247	262	277	292	307	322	337
203	218	233	248	263	278	293	308	323	338
204	219	234	249	264	279	294	309	324	339
205	220	235	250	265	280	295	310	325	340
206	221	236	251	266	281	296	311	326	341
207	222	237	252	267	282	297	312	327	342
208	223	238	253	268	283	298	313	328	343
209	224	239	254	269	284	299	314	329	344
210	225	240	255	270	285	300	315	330	345
211	226	241	256	271	286	301	316	331	346
212	227	242	257	272	287	302	317	332	347
213	228	243	258	273	288	303	318	333	348
214	229	244	259	274	289	304	319	334	349
215	230	245	260	275	290	305	320	335	350

something different . . .